6/91

CONTENTS

SUMMER OF BETRAYAL

1

4 JUNE 1989

SUNDAY

1

Tiananmen Square receded as she put it farther and farther behind her.

Lin Ying fled through a city alight with flames. Heavy gray gun smoke wrapped about her like mist, stinging her skin. Her face twitched, her hands shook uncontrollably. From time to time, her stomach turning, she staggered like a pendulum gone crazy. She ached to stop, lie down, vomit herself clean, but her legs disobeyed, dragging her forward. She kept on, one dash and then another and then another.

Surely this was a scene in some movie, a fabrication. Bloody battles like this happened only in nightmares. She had only to wake up, to call out with relief, "It's not true!" Right now the important thing was to hurry home to bed, to awaken in his arms and find that all of this hadn't happened.

Like a human tide, people dodging bullets had flowed into the alleys and lanes on the north side of the Avenue of Eternal Peace. After running first in one direction, then another, she found she was separated from anyone she knew. She dashed down a twisting lane that headed east, where the sound of gunfire seemed to be lighter.

When she thought she was out of danger, she suddenly found herself at a major boulevard. It was thick with soldiers, all wearing identical helmets, submachine guns at the ready, young faces covered with ashes and sweat, none showing a flicker of emotion. Tank after tank thundered by at measured speed. Anything in the way of the tanks was flattened or overturned: bicycles, carts, iron railings, buses. Vehicles were bursting into flames, shaking the earth and the sky and making the buildings on either side look as if made of paper, as if at any moment they might ignite and float heavenward. The smell of scorched asphalt assaulted the nose, mixed with the stench of burned bodies and blood.

Frightened shadows sped by.

She gripped the wall, not allowing herself to fall. Another string of footsteps pounded along from behind and a voice cried out, "Run!" A sharp instrument seemed to be twisting in her brain. She pulled herself together, then continued, hugging the wall to avoid bullets and never looking back. Only when the tanks and other people had passed and nobody was around did she allow herself to slow down. Dragging her exhausted body, she limped through smoke-filled streets like a dog being chased, sniffing the ground, trying to find a corner to hide in.

Must flag down a car. For the past few weeks, Lin Ying had gotten used to sticking out her hand and quickly getting an enthusiastic driver ready to give her a free lift. Now the streets were strewn with obstructions—buses, taxis, lorries overturned, smashed, twisted. Except for the tanks and the army trucks that followed right behind them, no vehicles were on the road.

Abandoned bicycles leaned against walls under the yellow streetlights, against trees, by the entrances to alleyways. Here before her eyes was a ready-made means of transportation, but Lin Ying, raised in a mountain city, had never learned how to ride a bicycle. She had regretted this in the year or so she had been in Beijing. "It can't be that hard," she muttered to herself now.

After the desperate flight through half the city, her body was rebelling. Her flesh and blood seemed congealed, as though she might shatter at any moment, crumble and fall around her own feet like pieces of plaster. "Really, what could be so hard about it?" At this second thin, hoarse utterance, she recognized her own voice.

Should she return to Balipu, to the dormitory where students in the university's writing program lived? Or to her own home, at Chen Yu's? No need even to ask. Chen Yu would be waiting for her, worried, standing by the telephone in case she called.

There was a telephone booth across the road. Reaching into her skirt pocket, she discovered that her purse had fallen out at some point, probably when she'd stumbled and fallen. Her wristwatch was also gone. She couldn't find any change to make a call. A coin would have been useless anyway, since most of the phone booths in the city were broken. She went on. A storefront displayed the symbol for public phones, but the door was locked. Her light-blue skirt was spattered with patches of someone's blood. The spots were coated over with mud that had dried and begun to crumble.

EARLY-MORNING light began to penetrate the smoke and haze in the streets. She was approaching a large traffic intersection in the east. She had put the sound of gunfire and burning behind her, to the west.

Faces began to reveal themselves behind windows and doors. People flitted through the little byways between buildings, between the clumps of shrubs and bushes along the road. Unconsciously she straightened her clothes, brushed back her shoulder-length hair, rubbed off the dirt and soot and sweat that streaked her face. Ready, she headed in the direction of human beings.

Those people who had hidden during the night now, at dawn, were venturing out to learn what had happened. Several army trucks, lined up neatly in a row, stood patiently in the middle of the road emitting heavy smoke. The soldiers had long since abandoned them. A number of people were throwing soda bottles into the flames, others were picking up empty gunshells. About a dozen people were standing silently near a mailbox and a parked three-wheeler. After a moment's hesitation, Lin Ying walked over to them. Unprepared, she abruptly caught sight of a body lying in a strange position on the sloping ground. One eye was bulging out like a small round ball; the other eye was squashed to a slit. Dark-red blood looked as though it had been deliberately splattered on the man's white undershirt, his blue underpants, his graying hair and beard. White brain matter mixed with blood seemed to be oozing onto the ground.

Lin Ying had run madly though the night, herself pursued by death. This was the first time she had seen the savagery of death in the light of day. Her stomach churned and this time doubled her up in pain. She pushed away from the crowd. Leaning against an electric pole at the sidewalk, she began to vomit. Her temples were throbbing, people and things whirled before her. She held tightly to the pole, panting and vomiting in turn. Whatever was still in her stomach after the night came out as thick, stinking bile. When she had emptied herself, an uncontrollable dry heaving continued.

A middle-aged woman stopped with her bicycle. "Young lady, what's the matter?" she asked, concerned.

Lin Ying struggled to lift her head and point to the people surrounding the corpse. The woman parked her bike and gently patted Lin Ying on the back. She looked like a worker. "That was an old widower," she said, "who shouldn't have come out on his balcony last night to see what was happening. He was hit by a stray bullet."

The touch of a human hand comforted Lin Ying. Supporting herself against the pole, she asked the woman for a ride to the Yellow Temple. Lin Ying felt she could walk no farther.

"Get on, little one, get on!" The woman got onto

her bicycle. "I can't go to work anyway. I'll take you. Oh my, what a sin! What a sin!" She kept repeating this as they rode along. "What they've done! What a mess they've made!"

Lin Ying sat on the back, holding on to the woman's waist. She shut her eyes, calmer now, the terror subsiding. The bicycle bounced as it went over bumps. Lin Ying opened her eyes to see the high gray walls of a building near the Yellow Temple, just visible on the street corner. She had the feeling that the striped curtains she knew so well were fluttering for her from every window. After a night of madness she would soon sleep.

3

Security was tight at the entrance to the *People's Daily* compound. A sentry post had been installed. The soldier on guard stopped and questioned Lin Ying. She said she lived there.

"Which block, which doorway?"

She specified the number. Fortunately the guard did not scrutinize her clothes—his gaze remained on her face. Finally, reluctantly, he let her in.

Trees lined both sides of the main entryway and marched down the endless avenue. Neatly mown lawns separated the trees and the buildings. Lin Ying staggered at each step. Just get to Chen Yu. He would hold her, take her in his arms, and put her to bed. Lie down. Be comfortable. He would bring her the milk with honey she loved so, then caress her and keep her company while she slipped into peaceful slumber. The day he had met her at the train station, he had said, "Little

Ying, my poor little thing, you need a good rest. When you've woken up, everything will be the way you want it to be.'' Gazing at Chen Yu back then, she had slowly closed her eyes and thought, From now on, I will no longer be tossed on the waves.

The boulevard was unnaturally silent, empty of people. A bird flew past, soundless, its wings stirring the still air. She passed a dry water fountain, her legs unbearably heavy. Whatever you do, don't stop, she told herself. Hold on. You'll be home in a minute. The word *home* was like a pool of light pushing back terrors, holding her securely in its warm depths.

Lin Ying finally went into one of the gray buildings. Each stairway landing was crowded with padlocked bikes and garbage cans. She climbed the stairs with difficulty, holding the bannister with her left hand while her right loosened a key chain tied around her neck. By the last flight of stairs, at the top of the building, she could hardly catch her breath, but her feet kept moving along the corridor to the first door. She inserted the key in the lock and turned it to the left three times. The door opened, she went in and shut it behind her.

She crossed the tiny entryway in five steps, past a small table, and pushed open the bedroom door.

The curtains were drawn. Chen Yu was lying on the bed in the darkened room. He must have waited for her all night and only now fallen asleep. Lin Ying could no longer stand, her body swayed, and she knew she was going to fall. If so, she should fall into his arms. She took a step toward the bed and collapsed beside it on the carpet. Her body went limp as her eyes closed and her head came to rest on his chest.

The clock on the wall ticktocked, back and forth.

"Yu," she called, almost silently. He had not woken. The only sounds seemed to come from her own pulse, her breathing, and the ticking of the clock.

Surely nothing had happened! With great effort, she forced her eyes open.

The room already seemed less dark. She now saw that Chen Yu was staring at her, that distress and horror filled his face.

Do I look so terrifying? Confused, she pushed against the bed as she brought her right leg underneath her and slowly raised herself up.

Chen Yu's head turned ever so slightly toward his back. Lin Ying's gaze automatically moved in that direction, and now she saw that something else was on the bed: a woman, her head buried in the bedding but some of her dishevelled hair showing, as well as part of her naked back. Chen Yu slowly pulled his hand out from under the woman's body.

Lin Ying sprang to her feet, speechless. She could not believe the fact before her eyes: Chen Yu in bed with another woman. Her entire being felt as if turned to ice; even the scream inside her was frozen.

Two hands of despair began pulling her inexorably backward, forcing her toward the door. Her eyes stayed fixed on Chen Yu, and only when she bumped against the door did she know she'd been moving. She turned abruptly and ran from the bedroom. The stool by the table clattered as she knocked it going through the hall. She pulled open the front door and took the stairs at a run. Outside the building, she stopped, panting, by the trees, their two straight green lines like soldiers at attention, holding rifles. Coming off parade, they now advanced toward her, step by step.

She shrank back, but behind her was a sheet of flames and smoke. The glowering sky darkened; gunfire, shouting, and the growl of tank engines merged in a cacophonous crescendo.

She had nowhere to run to.

4

Lin Ying heard Chen Yu saying her name, sometimes clearly, sometimes muffled, as she moved in and out of consciousness. Her clenched fist opened and she felt the rough fabric on the couch; only then did she realize where she was. Chen Yu was wiping her face with a damp towel. She pushed him away and tried to stand, but he held her down.

She fought back and struggled to sit up. Her feet found her sandals, covered with ashes inside and out. The green striped curtains of the window had been pulled open, but the room was still quite dark. The bed was made up with an ivory-colored bedspread. A woman in tight black pants sat on a chair opposite. She had short hair, the left side slightly longer than the right. Her eyes glittered in the darkness and she didn't say a word.

Clearly, this was the woman who had been lying in the bed. Lin Ying herself must have been carried back upstairs by Chen Yu. The whole recent scene had effectively stemmed the tears that should have come after her night of exhaustion and terror escaping from the shooting. What might have poured out was now returned to the deepest recesses of her mind. The only signs of what she had been through were her nostrils cracked with dryness and her painfully aching throat.

One nightmare had been followed by another; the stage was different, the actors were different, but the nightmares went on.

Lin Ying reached out both hands to a cup of tea on the table near the sofa. She drank one mouthful slowly, then all the rest. Her throat felt better. The other woman drew circles with her finger around the top of a glass ashtray. Chen Yu smoked, one cigarette after another. The smoke from his mouth, joining smoke drifting up from incompletely extinguished cigarette butts, screened the woman, blurring the contours of her body so that all Lin Ying really saw were her eyes.

Lin Ying straightened up, away from the back of the sofa. She brushed back a lock of hair and smoothed her short-sleeved jacket and skirt. She looked at the ashtray on the table and paused a moment, then reached out to take a cigarette from the pack. The tobacco was too strong—she took one drag, then let the cigarette smolder between her fingers. The three of them sat in silence, as though the air in the room were solid, as though the room were completely silted up.

Chen Yu's mouth twitched once, but he said nothing. His eyes were deep-sunken and bloodshot, and he looked as though he hadn't shaved in the several days Lin Ying had been away. He was haggard and thin, and his shirt was wrinkled.

In the end it was the other woman who broke the silence. "I've always wanted to meet you." She said this slowly and deliberately, in a light, low voice. Her daring to speak relaxed her; the two others in the room sat frozen. "I even dreamed of you a few times." She put her hands in her pockets, casually.

Lin Ying placed the filter of the burned-out cigarette

in the ashtray. She realized this was Mei Ling, the wife whom Chen Yu said he had been living apart from for two years and whom he was in the process of divorcing. In the year that Lin Ying had been living with Chen Yu in Beijing, she had never known them to have any contact, not even a phone call, let alone an actual meeting. When Chen Yu had talked of this unsatisfactory marriage, it was as though he were discussing educational materials in a course on the Communist Party. The only thing that remained between them, he said, was the final signatures on the divorce papers.

Lin Ying's face was ashen—not with jealousy, not with anger at any deceit, for she hadn't had time to think of these things. Instead, she felt total emptiness.

Chen Yu silently examined the glowing end of his cigarette. He hardly resembled the Chen Yu who had had her try on a wedding ring. He seemed far removed. Lin Ying became aware that what she wanted at this moment was not a man who loved her; what she wanted was an unshakable, immovable form of trust, the kind that could give stability in this upside-down world, an unchanging, steady diamond pivot.

She stood up and said softly, "I'm going."

Nobody objected.

Mei Ling also stood up, grinding out her cigarette. "Wait just a moment, I'll be going too."

Only Chen Yu continued to sit and smoke, without even looking up. The women seemed to have found the strength to act; he was left not knowing what to do.

Lin Ying took the key chain from around her neck and put it on the sofa. Woven of blue and green silk threads, it was something parents might hang around a child's neck, and when Chen Yu had first given it to her, she'd been overjoyed. Now it seemed vulgar—so clearly a trap, falsely pretending to be a symbol of home. Like other symbols, it said, Look, here I am! You should be satisfied! Lin Ying shook her head. Even now, her childhood hopes for life did not seem so outrageous: a lamp glowing at the window, a spot of yellow warmth in a lacquer-black expanse of wilderness.

Mei Ling looked at the keys, perplexed.

Lin Ying moved around the table with a determination that surprised even her. Without a word, without glancing at Chen Yu, she turned and left the room.

5

No shops were open on the streets, no vendors were hawking wares on the sidewalk. The occasional pedestrian hurried along. Bicyclists and peddlers with their three-wheeled carts kept their noses pointed straight ahead, their mouths open and breathing hard.

Lin Ying went through the central gate of the editorial department of the *People's Daily*. She walked in a daze along the road from the Yellow Temple in the direction of Balipu. After a while, she could no longer lift her feet. She leaned against a willow tree, then sat on the small ridge of earth beside the sidewalk.

A young person wearing sunglasses rushed past without stopping but called out to her, "Soldiers coming from that side. Quick, get out of here!"

Lin Ying didn't move. She couldn't move. If they are coming, let them come.

She might be able to endure Chen Yu's sleeping with other women. But that it was Mei Ling, the person Chen Yu said he most despised, was something else. He had said he couldn't tolerate her. That she was vain, superficial, ignorant, a chatterbox. Hearing all this, Lin Ying couldn't help being amused at first, but as the repetition of faults continued, she hadn't been sure what to believe.

If there had been no disaster last night, she might still be keeping vigil at the square, full of feelings like everyone else—happy, excited, indignant, hopeful—feelings that, good or bad, had to do with more than just her own self. Or if she'd fallen in the rain of bullets, none of the nightmare would have happened. Then she wouldn't have learned what sort of a person Chen Yu was. What age am I? she wondered. She had long since passed the age of girlish sentimentality and had encountered a fair dose of deceit. As a woman with knowledge of the bittersweet world, did she actually still believe that people had self-restraint? Did she still give any weight to love's promises? She should long ago have understood that lying and doing evil are the basic ways the world goes round.

The absurdity! That she could have hoped it would be into Chen Yu's arms that she finally collapsed!

Sitting at the side of the street, she hugged her knees, resting, then finally raised her head. Her hands tapped out a nervous rhythm on her knees. Stop thinking, she told herself, otherwise you'll go crazy. She prayed that fatigue would overcome her, mind and body.

The street was covered in dirt and in broadsheets and wall posters, ripped up and shredded. Pieces of them still stuck to walls, and the debris on the street had been squashed. At the corner was a burned-out army tank emitting its last wisps of smoke. Catty-corner, across the street, what had once been a public toilet was now a pile of broken bricks and rubble—perhaps smashed by a tank inadvertently.

Ten days ago Lin Ying had passed through this street and used this toilet. A group of female student demonstraters had been there, waiting in line, and even in the midst of the stench they had been singing happily—not the "March of the Volunteers" or "Blood-Dyed Grace" but a light happy tune:

Follow your feelings, hold tight to the hand of the dream.

She had felt happier and happier as she joined the girls in their song. Now this seemed years ago. Those fresh, rosy faces! She relaxed as she remembered, and suddenly she had to sleep, if only for a moment. Her eyes closed, and they couldn't open again.

SOMEONE WAS shaking her out of a deep slumber. A person was standing in front of her, bending over and staring, his mouth opening and closing as though he were saying her name. She lifted her head, forced her eyes open, rubbed them hard. It was Li Jiangjiang, a young literary critic she knew.

Li Jiangjiang's face was streaming with sweat, and he was out of breath as he shouted at her anxiously, "What are you doing here?"

Slowly Lin Ying stood up. She'd been running all night, she said, and now she wanted to go back to the university but she couldn't move another step, she had simply sat down here and gone to sleep.

"Can't go back to the writing program. Everyone

there is leaving. The Public Security Bureau has searched it. They arrested your classmate Yi Dafu."

Lin Ying stared at Li Jiangjiang. "Him? He's not one of the leaders. They're arresting everyone?" This was the first news she had heard of how things had developed since last night. Her voice was weak with shock. "Will they get everyone?" she said, not really asking Li Jiangjiang and certainly not herself.

"It was early this morning." Li Jiangjiang spoke rapidly. "Yan Yan called to tell me. The director told everyone who could to leave immediately. He said that the army would be moving in right away, that the canteen wouldn't be serving students anymore. Nobody knows for sure what's going to happen."

Lin Ying's eyes swept down the street. Smoke was still puffing from the tank on the corner. Now she truly felt like a startled bird in flight. It had only been an empty bunk at the school and she seldom slept in it; what's more, she had almost no personal belongings. Whatever she had was at Chen Yu's place but she did not want to go back and get it. In this big city suddenly there was not a single branch she could perch on.

"Come to our place. The Art Institute dormitory is pretty empty right now. Stay a few days, see how things develop, and then think about what to do. How about it?"

She hesitated. Li Jiangjiang added, "We're far from the center of the city—we're on the airport road, maybe a little safer. Your friend Hua Hua is also there."

His sincerity made Lin Ying feel that she had been a little too cautious. Not much older than she was, he was a man of slightly above-average height, with a high forehead and a boyish face. He had telephoned her once after she had arrived in Beijing to say he'd like to visit her; they'd set a time but had to cancel for some reason or other. Later they'd run across each other several times at poetry readings and said hello but never taken it further. She had a pleasant impression of him.

"Your bicycle doesn't have a rack." As she said it she knew she'd accepted. Circumstances did not allow for reflection.

"Sit on the frame in front." Li Jiangjiang held the handlebars steady. "You're too tired—sitting in front will be safer anyway."

6

Li Jiangjiang's voice floated up to her from behind. "The rack was broken by my old girlfriend. We'd bike to class together, to the library, to the cafeteria, sometimes to the outskirts of Beijing."

Lin Ying felt he was suggesting something, but she wasn't quite sure what it was. Anyway, it had nothing to do with her. Her eyelids drooped. The bumps in the road jolted her from sleep.

The bicycle twisted and turned through piled-up obstructions. Li Jiangjiang pedaled hard. Two broken-down streetcars blocked the road near Hujialou, and a pancake stand had been overturned in the pedestrian crossway. Broken eggs and flour were smeared all over, making a dark goo littered with pieces of shell. Lin Ying got off as Li Jiangjiang squeezed the bicycle in between the streetcars. She noticed that his denim shirt had gotten dirty.

He pulled Lin Ying back up onto the bike after clearing the obstacles and they went on.

The stretch of the Third Ring Road by the big overpass was deserted. They passed through without stopping. Li Jiangjiang's breath was heavy and damp on the back of Lin Ying's neck. Pumping hard, he occasionally brushed against her back. She had only to lean backward to feel his heart pounding.

They heard the high whine of a police car bearing down on them.

Li Jiangjiang kept pedaling without speeding up. Gunshots sounded close by, a popping sound, a bit like firecrackers. The screaming police siren pressed toward them and soon they saw the faceless black vehicle with its darkened windows. The bicycle lurched for a moment and Lin Ying almost slipped off, but she tightened her grip and sat firm. "Cover the blood on your skirt," Li Jiangjiang said tensely.

With one hand she whipped the skirt around to cover the worst of the stains as the car, screaming madly, flew past.

The intersection of San Yuan overpass was just behind them when Lin Ying's heart again jumped inside her. Around ten soldiers, submachine guns in hand, were marching in lockstep toward them.

"Don't be afraid."

Lin Ying swiveled around to look at Li Jiangjiang. He smiled at her. Since yesterday evening, she had been struggling alone—in this brief moment, she felt his support. Summoning up her courage, she looked again at the soldiers: helmets, uniforms tightly buttoned, rifles held ready at their chests, they marched down the center of the street, looked the two of them over, turned their gaze back to the overpass, and marched on.

The two of them drew a long breath.

T H E W A Y to the airport was straight. Trees and flowers had been planted along both sides of the road, row after row of tall white poplars and elms. Here and there was a patch of tended lawn or a flower bed. The air seemed brighter now, perhaps because there were no burning vehicles.

After the bus station at Seven Tombs, they came to a guard post at an intersection. There was no policeman inside, nor were there any cars on the road. Li Jiangjiang said, "That compound on the left is where our dormitory is."

"Just there?"

"It's the dorm for single people," he said. "The institute rents the building for graduates who are already working."

The first floor was deserted and all the doors along the hallway were closed. The second and third floors smelled of smoke: charred bits of paper fluttered in the passageways. People were sprinkling water on the floor and sweeping the debris toward the bathroom door. "Brother, burn what needs to be burned. Got to get it done quickly," Lin Ying heard a man say to Li Jiangjiang, who had gone into the bathroom. The sound of sobbing came from one of the rooms.

On the fourth floor the hall seemed to have just been given the same treatment. Li Jiangjiang opened the door to Room 414 and invited Lin Ying in. "First stay awhile here in my room. Rest a bit. There'll be food to eat, don't worry." He glanced at his watch and said he would go down to the canteen and look for Hua Hua, who might find a way to get Lin Ying somewhere to stay. He closed the door behind him as he left.

The room was filled with books. The shelves were full of them, and stacks of volumes were piled on a table by the wall. Prints of landscapes were taped all over—on the head of the bed and on the walls. The bed had a straw mattress; a pillow in a purple case showed the impression of a person's head, but it wasn't dirty. A folded pale yellow washcloth lay on a corner of the bed. Lin Ying took it all in: not bad for a bachelor. It wasn't so messy that you couldn't find a place to put your feet. An alarm clock on the table said two o'clock.

What does two o'clock mean? she wondered. What day is this?

When she sat down on the bed her body simply slumped backward. It would no longer obey her mind. How long had it been since she had slept, eaten, or drunk anything? The calculation was too difficult: time had been shredded by the course of events. She tried to work it out, to set aside what had happened to her and think only of the raw, abstract arithmetic of what time it might be. But sleep pressed out memory and thought alike. She soon succumbed to a deep, heavy slumber.

7

Without opening her eyes, Lin Ying became aware that it was dark around her. Her eyes stayed closed; she couldn't seem to open them. A shortwave radio was broadcasting something. The announcer's deep voice came through the crackle of interference as though it were her own, as though, half asleep, she were talking to herself: ". . . today at dawn . . . Beijing's Tiananmen Square . . . tanks . . . numbers are as yet unclear . . . according to reports . . . burning . . . President Bush . . ."

She shut her eyes tighter, then finally opened them. It was in fact already dark outside. Li Jiangjiang was sitting at the desk with the lamp turned very low. He was adjusting the dials on the radio, trying to get a connection through the static. Faint bursts of gunfire could be heard in the distance, and from time to time came a concentrated muffled burst. The odd single gunshots were much clearer. His head down, Li Jiangjiang concentrated on the radio. He switched to an English station with slightly less interference, but the sporadic words that made it through were even less intelligible: ". . . lines of demonstrators . . . arms raised . . . a barrage of shooting . . . slogans . . . army trucks . . ." Like water, the words flowed in and out of her mind.

Every flagstone, every single stone. The stones had been connected by a deep red. She had never seen such redness. When she touched it, it dissolved in her fingers into glittering beads of red light. The raking sound of gunfire, da-da-da, was all around her. Which way should she run? Down which street? She fled, crouching, over the flagstones, the redness flowing beneath her.

Crumpled tents were everywhere, flags fallen to the ground, clothes, shoes, the wailing of voices crying out in horror. Flares and tracer bullets danced crazily in the air. She looked back. Her footsteps shone distinctly in the redness between earth and heaven, describing an erratic curve that led all the way back into darkness. Tanks were now speeding along that path.

She wanted to stand up, stand in the way of the rolling line of vehicles, use her own small body to block their way. She wanted to cry out, "You can't kill people!" but she was too terrified to make a sound.

Sheets of bullets whizzed by. The soldiers' uniforms were so green, the five red stars on their hats and collar insignias were so brilliantly crimson. She could run no longer, she stumbled and fell. She tried to stand but tripped again. The dark red ground traced the contours of her body, sucking her down as the treads of the heavy tanks rolled closer. She screamed.

"Lin Ying, wake up! Wake up!" Li Jiangjiang was leaning over the head of the bed, calling to her. She sat up and propped herself against the wall. The bottom corner of the curtain was fluttering in the breeze, the radio in the room was still on—no station, just crackling static.

"You were talking in your sleep, shouting," Li Jiangjiang said. "Have something to eat. I've left dinner for you."

Lin Ying shook her head.

"It rained hard this afternoon. Hua Hua never came back." Li Jiangjiang was trying to be calm. "I just hope nothing's happened."

Happened? What kind of thing? The words seemed to prod every sore muscle in her body. Her brain felt cut in two: half was watching the wheels of the tanks, looming larger as they rolled closer; half saw a man with a strange face that looked like Chen Yu's, though it was hard to tell for sure. From opposing directions, tanks and man charged at each other, folding into each other, becoming a gigantic fireball whirling through the sky.

Eyes staring wide, she screamed. Once, then again.

A pair of strong arms gripped her. Hot tears rolled down her cheeks.

8

In the darkness, her clothes slipped off a body that was empty and translucent.

Li Jiangjiang's lips moved gently on her face, kissing her. His fingers moved from her shoulders to her breasts. His hands and his lips were quivering uncontrollably. She felt his hair brush her face, her neck. The bristles around his lips prickled her skin; each new place they touched drew a little involuntary gasp.

Take him as a man or as a kind of possibility?

A wisp of cloud began to float in from the distance and accumulate in the center of the room. It came from long ago, from the ocean at Beibuwan. What was it I heard once, in some telephone call? I missed you before and now have met you again. A tear fell on her face, then another, which joined the flow of her own tears. How could a man use tears to take her heart? Dark red flows through the lanes and from the streets. The smell of corpses rising in the air. She buried her head in Li Jiangjiang's chest, trying to escape a terror that stole her breath.

Just then the pounding rumble of a line of armored vehicles sounded in the street outside. It shook the building, rattled the glass in the windows, made the metal of the bed clank. Lin Ying and Li Jiangjiang clung to each other as they moved closer to the wall, their mouths open, gasping for air. Army vehicles were entering the city in a steady stream. At any moment bullets might come through the curtains.

She pushed him away suddenly. Terror and a feeling of powerlessness instantly returned. Was there not a single small island of safety in this violently insane world? Despair, that most ruthless of emotions, gave her no room for doubt. She threw herself into Li Jiangjiang's arms again, her body curled tightly in his. Everything that had happened flickered frame by frame before her: the flow of people running, flames lighting the sky, the maimed bodies, and then that ash-gray building with Chen Yu and Mei Ling embracing.

To be assaulted twice in one day made her furious now, and in her fury her naked body trembled. Her fingernails clawed at Li Jiangjiang, her heart contracted till it was like a shrill little mouse squeaking in distress. She had to grab onto something, anything at all; what it was or whether or not it belonged to her made no difference.

Every physical sensation seemed heightened. Chen Yu? No need to think of him. She was not responsible for him, just as she was not responsible for her own life or for what came next . . . just as she could not be blamed for the burning of the city.

The sharp whine of police cars outside, piercing the grind and roar of army trucks, pressed forward, like a sin.

Her breasts yielded to the pressure of his fingers. The muscles inside her gripped him in a frenzy, their bodies rising and falling till she heard a high-pitched singing cry accompanying her own grieving shout.

The city had fallen.

As though hit by a bullet, she suddenly knew nothing at all.

9

A hubbub of sounds contended within Lin Ying's head: footsteps in the hallway, the long-long, short-short ring of the telephone, an upset voice answering, honks on the road outside. Some people seemed to be discussing something very urgently. Somebody finally yelled, "Canteen's open! Food at last!"

She didn't want to open her eyes. She wasn't sure what she would do with herself if she let go of the darkness. Someone knocked on the door; no one answered. She felt around with her hands to discover that she was sleeping alone on the single bed.

"Jiangjiang." A hoarse male voice called from the outside as the pounding on the door continued.

Only then did she remember that this bed was not her own. She opened her eyes. She was still cocooned in darkness and Li Jiangjiang was gone. The clock on the table still said two o'clock. So maybe it had been wrong from the start. She stretched over and reached for Li Jiangjiang's wristwatch on the table. Already five-thirty. How could it be five-thirty? Confused, she threw aside the bedcover, raised herself up, and pulled back the closed curtains. The sky outside was purple tinged with yellow.

Sitting up now, she saw food left for her on the chair: a dish of eggplant and a plate of scrambled eggs. Also a note: "Lin, you're so tired you haven't woken yet. When you have, eat something right away. If you feel like it, come to Room 5104, in the back of Building A this evening. I have to go out. Jiangjiang. 5 June, afternoon."

The note had been tucked under a small package. Opening it, she found a clean washcloth wrapped around a new toothbrush and a bar of soap. Suddenly aware of the smell of her body, the dirt under her fingernails, the grime between her toes, she stood up, dressed, and opened the door. Her legs stiff, she headed down the hall toward the sound of water. After a few steps, she realized she had no clean clothes to change into. She went back and found a white shirt and a pair of gym shorts that Li Jiangjiang had left to dry in the corner. She also picked up a basin, then went to the public lavatory to take a bath.

After washing, she stood before the mirror, smoothing back her hair. The Lin Ying in the mirror—water beading her face, deep-sunken eyes ringed by lines of fatigue, desolation on her forehead and at the corners of her mouth—she had never seen before. Her neck was bruised and she couldn't hold her thin shoulders straight.

Is this me or is it a ghost? She stared a long time, and finally the person revealed a few teeth back at her, a grim smile with the mouth pulled to the left. Then she put on Li Jiangjiang's clothes. The sleeves were too long, so she rolled them back till her wrists showed. The hem came down over her rear, almost covering the short gym pants.

Back in Li Jiangjiang's room, she turned on the lamp and poured herself a mug of hot water from the thermos. She gulped down the cold food like a famished animal. With food and two cups of hot water, her hunger subsided, but now pain came on again. Her nerves were stretched as tight as a lute string ready to vibrate at the slightest pluck. She turned off the lamp, wanting to sit quietly for a moment. The past, the present, the future—a book that had been ripped to shreds. Where should she start in order to put everything together again?

Tonight, I am here. Since I'm here, I don't need to be absolutely clear about every single thing, she told herself. These past few months, life had been more intense than at any time before, packed with events and news that filled the streets, the whole square, the whole city. Minor personal affairs had been superseded by great national events. Now only she remained. She didn't quite know what to do with herself. But she knew she couldn't stay in the darkness alone.

She stood up and got ready to look for the room Li Jiangjiang had mentioned in his note. Just to have a look.

A telephone sat on a stool at the head of the stairs; the endless ringing she had heard in her dreams must have come from it. She picked up the receiver and without thinking dialed an old familiar number. It rang six times. Nobody answered.

What am I doing? Flinging down the receiver, she stood facing the wall. Did you think you had put it behind you? You can't be so weak—you're just asking for ridicule.

10

She did not know Li Jiangjiang well. His poetry criticism was trenchant, incisive, he always had something new and clever to say, and whenever she heard he had written something, she would look for it and read it. She found his writing style overblown, full of unpronounceable words expounding on deep mysteries—she thought it would be much more effective to say things simply. Still, people who write poetry cannot readily criticize critics of poetry. She always paid her respects to theory and kept her distance.

In fact, they had met only briefly, at the 1987 poetry conference at Beibuwan, in Guangxi Province. Then, she had sensed that Li Jiangjiang was watching her when she was in a group of people. She was accustomed to this kind of attention and didn't find it bothersome, but she also didn't consider it a compliment. Every time she looked around she saw him turn the other way and pretend to be looking at something else. A big child.

He had been rising rapidly in the two years since, having published a collection of critical essays. He touched on abstruse topics and used terms like *épater epoché* and *différance illimitée*, making people feel they had nothing to say and should be ashamed of being so stupid. He once asked Lin Ying, "Why don't you ever ask me to review your poetry?" People who wanted to become famous as writers had to win the praise of critics, which didn't get you the same power as winning official prizes but worked nevertheless—official poets and unofficial ones went their own ways.

Lin Ying had answered, "Why don't you ask me to *allow* you to review my poetry?"

Both had laughed and left it at that. Lin Ying never asked and, true to his word, he never reviewed her.

Last night, in her extreme fatigue, the man to comfort her and save her should have been Chen Yu. Instead it was this Li Jiangjiang, toward whom Lin Ying did not feel remotely romantic. If God existed, he was either a madman or a perverse child.

LIN YING found Building A beyond the garden and trees, past the canteen.

She climbed to the fifth floor. The corridor lights were dim and only one of the rooms was open. From it streamed a commotion of voices. An acrid, nose-stinging smell of cigarette smoke intensified as she approached.

She stepped to the door. Lots of people were crowded inside, some seated on the bed, some standing, some sitting on the floor. A long fluorescent lamp made everyone look pallid. Several of them, their voices overwrought, were on the verge of tears. A shortwave radio seemed to be tuned to the BBC. Eyes were red, whether from crying or the smoke.

Lin Ying sat by the door, avoiding the heavy air inside and the worst of the cigarettes. At the end of the corridor, there were other people crying and talking by a window.

Li Jiangjiang came out and lightly put his arm around her. "You made it. Did you get something to eat?" His voice was neither ardent nor cool, as though nothing had happened between the two of them the night before.

Lin Ying nodded. "Who are all these people?"

"Most are from the Art Institute," Li Jiangjiang said. "Some are from the university. Perhaps you saw them at the square. They've been paralyzed for a couple of days—they're only just recovering. This is Hua

Hua's room; she only got here this morning. Everyone was worried about her, thought she was gone—and decided to get together on account of her being back."

"They all ran. I couldn't find a single one," someone was shouting. "The leaders ran and we pawns just got left behind, waving flags and shouting."

Another voice: "I never thought that those bastards would open fire, that they'd point straight at people and shoot them dead!"

Someone else was loudly indignant. "You should have thought of that a while ago. It was only you fucking sons of cunts who didn't know it. Politics in China isn't fucking rubber bullets."

"The dead are dead. Those who ran away are gone. So what do we do now?" A small man in a flowered shirt who was squatting on the floor said this with a sob in his voice. Nobody answered the question. A few people told him to sit on a chair that had become vacant. He ignored them. It was Yan Yan, a poet Lin Ying knew. His hair and beard were disheveled and he looked sick, holding a hand on his stomach. Frowning, he stared at each person in turn as though they were trying to cheat him.

The same question had probably been asked many times, and Yan Yan's was quickly superseded by other voices. The radio changed to a broadcast in Chinese and the room quieted down. A young woman wearing jeans and a sympathizer's shirt jumped up and ran over to hug Lin Ying.

"Lin Ying, little Lin, you're alive!" she shouted.

Lin Ying had never liked the theatrical way that Hua Hua talked. This time, though, she was not even aware of it. Everyone in the room was a friend who had just escaped death. She was demonstrative herself, grabbing Hua Hua's hand and asking, "How did you make it?"

There was a torrent now from Hua Hua: how she'd run into a dead-end lane and couldn't get out, how it was full of soldiers and she'd crouched in a corner, planning various escapes but unable to do anything. A little boy had opened the door to his house and pulled her inside. His parents made her stay with them in hiding for two days, letting her out only when it seemed a little safer.

"He was such an adorable little boy!" Hua Hua said.

Lin Ying couldn't understand how Hua Hua could seem so lighthearted when so many people had been killed and everybody's mood was so grim. She glanced angrily at Li Jiangjiang, who was staring at her.

Hua Hua seemed to know what she was thinking. "All I could think about at the time was the urgency, the terror, the anger, the tears. Now, seeing all these people, I've calmed down a little."

Lin Ying and Hua Hua had not seen each other much, but from the beginning they'd been like old friends; at least Hua Hua treated Lin Ying as an old friend whenever she spoke to her. She was studying drama at the Art Institute but it was clear that she should simply be an actress instead. Tall and slender, she had an enormously expressive face. She was intelligent, too, and there were few people, male or female, who didn't like her.

Li Jiangjiang had mostly been listening but now he said, "So when we went looking for Hua Hua last night, we couldn't find her. Otherwise you could have come to sleep here."

Hua Hua was confused for a moment but quickly caught on. Her mouth twitched as she said, "I see, and now you don't have to come stay here after all, right? Jiangjiang, you filthy thing, taking advantage of a damsel in distress!"

"Don't be so sure you've got it right," Lin Ying wanted to say. She hadn't had time to think over what had happened between her and Li Jiangjiang, but it had nothing to do with amorous feelings on either side. She was about to say something when the room became silent. The Chinese Voice of America program was announcing that they were interviewing a young Chinese writer, just arrived in San Francisco from Beijing, about the events in Tiananmen Square and on the Avenue of Eternal Peace on the night of 3 June. Several people in the room shouted, "It's got to be Daguang, the bastard!"

Someone told them to be quiet and nobody else spoke. They listened as the young writer described the terrifying hail of bullets on the Avenue of Eternal Peace that night. There was nothing special or remarkable about his experience. The experiences of most everyone in the square had been bloodier and more dangerous than his. He didn't say anything new, and it was all very simple, over in a few minutes. At the end, he said that it was terrifying to think about it again and that he was worried for the safety of his friends still in Beijing.

The announcer came on and explained that this had been the first opportunity to hear someone who had personally witnessed the events in Beijing. Then he turned to other developments, saying that there had been reports of mutinous army divisions in Beijing, that conflicts had arisen in the army command. There was a burst of furious rebuttals: "Idiots! How can they report that? Didn't they pass on enough fucking groundless rumors? Every single regiment followed orders, sons of bitches!"

One lividly angry voice stood out: "That bastard. So he becomes a hero, the whole world hanging on his personal story. Let the rest of us shed the blood!" The man charged toward the door, maybe just upset that so many were talking and nobody was listening to him. Lin Ying saw that it was Wu Wei, the literary editor of Beijing's leading newspaper.

Wu Wei saw her but didn't even nod as he continued his tirade. Normally he spoke with considerable sophistication, but not now. "The son of a bitch flew the coop. On the evening of the third, after the shooting had started, I called him. His plane ticket, passport, visa must have been prepared in advance. Maybe his luggage was packed and ready to go. But he didn't give the slightest hint to me! What kind of fucking 'brother' is that!"

"Wasn't it arranged a while ago for him to attend a Chinese cultural conference in America?" Lin Ying remarked.

"But what did he say that night? 'Looks as if I won't be able to make it,' he said! And 'Who cares?' "

"Do you mean that if you couldn't leave he shouldn't be allowed to go either?" Hua Hua put in.

Lin Ying felt a little sorry for Wu Wei. He was upset. "Didn't they say the airport never closed down, even in all this? Don't be so hard on a person."

Wu Wei didn't seem to hear either Lin Ying or Hua Hua. He paced back and forth in the corridor, his glasses nearly slipping off his nose, spit flying as he yelled, " 'Won't be able to make it'! What kind of 'sacrifice to the death' for the country was that, what kind of iron brotherhood?"

"Quiet down. All he said was, 'Looks like I won't be able to go,' " Hua Hua interrupted. "Don't forget where we are—heaven may be high here, but the emperor isn't far away. Maybe you haven't heard the new regulation: you have to apply for permission from the Public Security Bureau if you have a meeting of more than five people."

Yan Yan, who had been sitting vacantly in a corner, suddenly seemed shaken out of a dream. "Everything is fate!" he shouted. "China simply has a black fate!" He stood up and reached out his arms. "Black: the darkness of an iron cell!" He turned and sat down again in the corner without saying another word.

Lin Ying asked Li Jiangjiang, "What's going on with those constant police cars?"

"I heard there's a big prison east of here. This is the only road to it. They've evidently arrested a lot of people these past two days." Li Jiangjiang touched her shoulder. "Don't worry."

Lin Ying looked again at the crowded room. "There seem to be quite a few people from the Degraded Survivors' Club here."

Wu Wei heard her. "Degraded Survivors! Prophetic term! Right now everyone's going to have to be disgraced to survive. Some will make it famously—they've already made it to the Golden Gate Bridge. We here still don't know how we're going to make it." He was shouting again, but not as loudly.

People kept coming in and out of the room, and Li Jiangjiang and Hua Hua eventually went in. Only Lin Ying stayed outside by the doorway. Her mood had improved as she saw friends, but when Wu Wei said this she grew sober again. How lucky if a person could forget his own concerns and attend only to others. Sadly, she lacked this bit of good fortune. Everyone here was frightened. They had just experienced the worst tragedy in their young lives—and it brought them together, to cry together. But what she had encountered was not something she could tell the others; it was something no one else would understand.

A bearded man approached Lin Ying and put a hand on her shoulder. Looking up, she saw it was Yan Heituo, in an army uniform faded from washing, no insignia, cuffs rolled up to the elbows—the fashionable look among rock-and-roll singers.

"Hey, Lin Ying. So you're okay!" His voice was deep, his accent pure Beijing, slithery smooth as could be. He took in the man's shirt she was wearing, her bare legs. His eyes raked her body from the feet up to her face.

Lin Ying gave him an exasperated look. She never used to be irritated by this kind of attention, but here and now it made her uncomfortable. Turning away from him, she said lightly, "No problem," then added, "How did you get out of it all?"

"I didn't go out that night," Yan Heituo said candidly. "I stayed hidden in one of the foreigners' hotels. For the time being, they're not going to attack *there*!"

"You're pretty good at finding places to hide," Lin Ying said acidly.

Yan Heituo chuckled to cover his embarrassment. "All right, all right. It's hard for anyone who escaped along that bloody road to be in good humor. But, Lin Ying, what's with these clothes . . ."

"At a time like this! You're really something." Lin Ying knew that Yan Heituo considered himself a loner who liked to think, talk, and act differently from other people. But he was treating things as if they were normal. She couldn't bear it.

"A time like this is precisely the time to talk straight." Yan Heituo indicated the smoke-filled room. "Look, it's a mess in there. Overwrought. Any more of that highbrow theory and it may get even worse. The saying that 'metaphysical talk ruins the country' applies to exactly the kind of people in there."

"So you're all for saving the country, a rock-and-roll patriot?"

"First I have to save myself." He gestured at his army uniform. "See? I was supposed to be performing for foreigners tonight at the Hilton. But they were so scared they packed up and took off for the airport. Best I could do was to get a lift in their car and come here. Funny how their lives seem to be worth so much, while we seem to leave it all up to fate."

A tall woman picked her way slowly through the room, weaving in and out of the crowd of people. Yan Heituo blocked the door. "Shao Liuliu," he said, "don't go yet—there's still something to come."

"Ah, my esteemed colleague, so good you remembered—dancing on the corpses." She looked at Lin

Ying without saying hello, then walked away. Suddenly she turned back and said to Yan Heituo, "You're always mixing with the foreigners. Why don't you get one of them to take you abroad?"

"Why not?" Yan Heituo said. "To tell the truth, there've been several—women—trying to wrap me up in a suitcase and ship me out of the country. But you know, I never liked the idea."

Shao Liuliu lifted her thumb at Yan Heituo. "A time like this and all you think about is not being kept by a woman. What a tough fellow! I'd go at once with whoever got me a visa—pockmarked, crippled, anyone."

Someone in the room was shouting, "We'll just wait and see who survives whom!" Hua Hua could be heard above the others. "Hold on. Weren't you all looking for me to see if I was still alive? Don't cry so much, okay?" She pulled a bottle of wine out of a cupboard. Most of the people were still shouting protest slogans. Someone yelled, "Put on the 'Internationale'! Let's sing the 'Internationale'!" But Hua Hua turned on the tape player and slipped in a tape. The sound of light music began. Some retreated into the corridor to continue their agitated conversations, others stayed where they were. Lin Ying saw that Hua Hua was saying something to Yan Yan; they were each holding a glass of wine.

Yan Heituo took Lin Ying's hand. "Not easy to find a chance to see you," he said.

"All I want is a place to sit down with them all and do some more crying," was Lin Ying's response.

Yan Heituo let go of her hand. "Can't you see these people are hopeless? Literary types. No power, no plans—all they do is play with their pens! Cry about what? Right now we should be celebrating, ecstatic that we haven't been flattened!''

Lin Ying sensed that something was not altogether right about this way of thinking, but she couldn't figure out what. The music in the other room had switched to a different beat, and she was relaxing. Maybe he was right: at least the music calmed her pounding heart.

Someone turned out the overhead light. The desk lamp and the light from the corridor shone dimly on the people still in the room. The music seemed to flow among them. In the haze of tobacco smoke, the flickering scene looked like something from an old movie.

The corridor, in contrast, was filled with argument. People were planning new opposition slogans, plotting how to hang them on the doors of the Art Institute during the night. Someone was cutting up a black T-shirt, saying he intended to hang it on the tree at the end of the street as a memorial for the dead. Voices rose and fell. Lin Ying moved a little into the room, leaning against the wall by the door.

The music changed to Ma Sicong's "Thinking of Home," sentimental and sad. Ma had written this piano piece during the War of Resistance against the Japanese, when he was far from home in the southwest, Lin Ying's home. Its heartrending tunes spoke of those who had lost their homeland, and every time she heard it she trembled inside. How could the hardships they had suffered there generation after generation come to nothing? This most famous of China's composers had braved death to swim to Hong Kong during the Cultural Revolution.

She closed her eyes. A wine bottle shattered on the floor.

Wu Wei shouted from the corridor, "Music! You're playing fucking music! You slimy degenerates! You're drunk, you're living in a dream!" He turned his back on them but seemed thoroughly drunk himself. He was staggering.

Suddenly the shrill sirens of security cars howled. Terror instantly obliterated the little haven. Everyone stopped talking. No one knew what to do. Only the music kept flowing serenely, as if ridiculing their heroic posturing in the face of imminent danger just a moment ago.

Softly Lin Ying began to giggle. She covered her face with her hands, but the room was too dark for anyone to notice her anyway. Her shoulders shook, and tears streamed through her fingers and down her cheeks.

2

I

Bare legs stepping into a roadside ditch to soak aching
feet. Dirt from between her toes flowing away with the
water. However much her shoulders and legs hurt,
she'd still have to keep on working, hauling sand from
the river. First you dumped a load of sand, sixty-five
pounds of it, into two carrying baskets and lifted them
with a shoulder pole. Then the two-hour climb up a
steep, narrow winding path to the construction site at
the top of the ridge. For each trip, you got twenty *jen.**

The steps of the mountain path stretched endlessly
above. Densely clustered houses on stilts lined both
sides of the path, their wooden walls long since mil-
dewed to the same gray as the roofs; no color anywhere.
Below, covered in the thick mist of low rain, was the

* One hundred *jen* make a *yuan*, equivalent roughly to 12 cents.

Yangtze. On the opposite bank was another mountain, beyond that more mountains, closing one in, constricting the line of vision.

She hoisted her carrying pole and resumed the climb up the zigzagging stone stairs. From time to time she would stop to catch her breath and wipe the sweat from her face. For half of the year this place was as hot and humid as an ant's nest.

Some nights she had flown over the river in her dreams, circling the city, floating high above the Revolutionary Heroes' Memorial in the city's center. A pair of outstretched wings had carried her countless times away from this land where she was born. If I ever leave, I'll never look back, she always said to herself.

Now the mountain city she had daily dreamed of leaving was thousands of miles away. And now, with great clarity, wide awake, she knew she had been wrong. She had left her homeland behind without nostalgia, but her homeland had clung tenaciously to the back of her mind.

Boats plied the river, their steam whistles calling over the water. On the opposite bank people were moving about on the landing. Vaguely one could see the docks and then laborers like her slowly climbing up the other side. A cable trolley going up the mountain there had long since broken and had never been fixed. A wooden raft floated down on the current, the oarsman in a straw hat carefully watching the eddies before him. The river would pour out of the gorges, pass through endless plains, then finally join the wide ocean. Perhaps there, at last, the sky was clear and blue, seagulls called, white sails danced on billows under the setting sun.

Her reflection wavered in the water: patched clothes,

two thin braids hanging in front of her shoulders, hair yellowed from malnutrition. Nobody in her class at school would speak to her. Before and after class she was bullied. She was scared of going to school.

Her father, a dockworker, had hurt his back and for years now had stayed at home. The family depended on the temporary jobs her mother took, washing clothes for people and cleaning. Sometimes she would have to take a job far away and be gone for weeks at a time. When her mother fell ill from exhaustion, conditions got even worse: then there was only her father's minuscule disability allowance, barely enough for two, which had to stretch to feed a household of five.

In those days you could see a movie for five *fen*, but she had never been to one. Years later, she realized, not without pleasure, that it was through lack of those *fen* that she had managed to avoid being indoctrinated by the movies of the time and their fake and vacuous "teaching." She was the eldest of the three children. Her father had ordered her to work to make money to help support the family. The only way to do so was to cut back on school. She tried her best to squeeze time for class—but once she was there, the characters on the blackboard would blur together, her head would drop on the desk, and she would be sound asleep, her mouth open.

Her father and mother fought constantly. With any alcohol in him, her father's temper would erupt. The family lived in a single room then, sharing a kitchen with the family next door: the room would be tense with the threat of violence. He would order the three daughters around and at the slightest mistake on their part would hurl the family's chopsticks to the floor. He knew that he couldn't start breaking bowls, but he would hit whoever was nearest him. At these moments her mother, who usually complained endlessly, would sit numb and immobile, just watching.

She learned a song in music class: "Wide, wide river, waves so gentle, breezes waft the fragrance of sweet rice along the banks. My home is there on the riverbank heights in the midst of sunlight shining bright." She sang it over and over again, intoxicated with the words, in order not to see the dingy grayness before her eyes. The humid air was thick with soot; the stench of sewage permeated the cities on either bank.

At night a familiar episode would often waken her. She would dream of falling into destitution and being chased, then her wings would be coming apart, pieces of them floating together with her in a freefall. When she woke, her mother's breasts and father's scrawny legs would be rocking outside the bedcovers. She would curl up tightly and silently turn the other way. One sister slept beside her, another slept crosswise at their feet. The ceiling was low and the wooden windows were kept tightly shut; the air had a permanent odor of something that had died—almost certainly more than one rat was rotting behind the walls. Narrow wooden steps that led from the door down to the street creaked noisily whenever they were stepped on.

Her pallid face was slightly jaundiced; her body was a thin rack of bones. But her breasts were swelling like round ricecakes in a steamer, erect and sore against her dress. She was terrified about this and didn't dare tell her mother. Her mother might scold her for being a low-class, filthy good-for-nothing. She secretly bound herself with a cloth, wrapping herself so tightly she could scarcely breathe.

Alone at the riverside, she would unbind the cloth and breathe deeply. With her face into the wind she could feel the rough, cool grit of sand on her cheeks and neck. The vast waters, covered with floating garbage, were sweeping—immutably, unalterably—by her feet.

A THIN, short boy often sat on a rocky point on the far bank, like her, just staring at the water. He, too, had a carrying pole and bamboo baskets for carrying sand. From the first day she discovered him there, everything was decided. It was inevitable: they were so much like each other. Only years later did she learn that she had not been sitting there without purpose, accepting the futility of a barren, ignorant life. She was waiting for change, for the chance to escape this generation-after-generation cycle of bitterness. This purpose was not concrete but stubbornly it led her forward.

2

Lin Ying stayed in the dormitory of the Art Institute for eleven days. The people in the writing program were like a flock of sparrows that had suddenly abandoned its tree. Everyone had disappeared; not a single person remained. She had telephoned a young teacher, Nan An, to ask about progress on the long-planned graduate course.

Nan An said nobody had told him it would be canceled, but then nobody had said there was any chance of its being held either. He suggested that Lin Ying not sit around and wait, that she go home to her family.

Lin Ying did not want to go home. It had been extremely difficult to pass the exam for the university and to struggle this far. She wasn't going to admit defeat so easily. Nor was there anywhere else she could go. She had no alternative but to wait here.

The staff people at the Art Institute who had not fled still had to go to the office every day to study Party instructions and the speeches that Central Committee leaders were making about the "disturbance." Lin Ying was often left alone in the room, looking through the stacks of Li Jiangjiang's books. Shrill police cars, one after another, shuttled back and forth on patrol in the streets, making it absolutely clear that this was a city under the tight control of gun barrels. The intent of the sirens was to make people insecure, to take away their appetite, to make it hard for them to rest easy—to agitate them so that they would eventually spill out their hearts and minds to the authorities, to wash themselves clean.

She often thought of the eyes of a wolf that she had seen in a dream.

> Swallow a grass seed, green grass grows inside you
> But what puzzles me more is the way
> The sun passed over my body this morning
> And lit upon the eaves.

What lines! Lin Ying threw down her pencil. Writing poems used to be the most natural thing in her life.

Now the words wouldn't come together: her notebook was filled with fragments of disjointed sentences. When history is calamity, she thought, perhaps poems could only be splinters of words, for traumas destroy normality.

After eating lunch alone, she sat on the only chair in Li Jiangjiang's room. A cup of hot water was on the table beside her. She leaned forward a little to face the slightly open window. Covering it was a nylon mosquito netting fastened to the eight squares of an iron grating. The sun shone in obliquely, casting a grim shadow of prison bars on the floor. She covered her eyes with one hand; the other gripped her skirt. If writing could no longer help her cleanse herself, then she would empty herself, let the wind blow over this empty water jug. She leaned back against the chair, her eyes shut, hands following the contours of her body, moving up the inside of her legs.

The air was hot and dry. The scorching summer days to come were already getting more and more real.

"What was there between you and Chen Yu?" Li Jiangjiang had asked in a general sort of way.

"You want to know?"

"I do."

A gibbous moon hung in the sky. Li Jiangjiang's hand had combed through Lin Ying's hair. When his fingers softly reached her neck, the coolness of the moon came into her through them.

"He always called me 'Yingzi,' Little Shadow. He liked me to tie a silk ribbon around my neck. Partly it was a superstition about covering the mole there, and it also made my neck look longer, more elegant.* His eyes would soften then as if there were a film over them." Lin Ying suddenly stopped.

The two of them sat still for a while, rigid.

Li Jiangjiang finally said, "You still love him, don't you?"

Lin Ying chewed her lower lip. It was hard to talk about something she couldn't make sense of. "You made me say these things. Anyway, the two of us made love, that's how it was."

"And what about me?" Li Jiangjiang asked.

"You and I can't be put into words. We're in search of beauty, like right now." She grabbed his arm, used her mouth to seal his lips, stop him from talking.

The door to the stairwell slammed; there were always people passing by outside their room.

Even when they lay quietly they had to press against each other, the bed was so narrow.

Li Jiangjiang said, "I loved someone once. She was a tiger year."

"I'm tiger year too." Lin Ying's voice.

"We made love in the ocean." As if in a dream, Li Jiangjiang told about his childhood playmate. Her parents had been arrested and taken away during the Cultural Revolution, so she was raised by her grandfather. They lost touch with each other for eleven years but unexpectedly ran into each other again at Nandaihe, by the ocean.

"She still wore her hair in braids, just like before. Her black bangs were straight and even on her fore-

---

* The Chinese superstition has it that a mole on one's throat is a mark that bodes ill, that one may die by hanging.

head. She had on a wet bathing suit, stood there smiling at me. Her toes had been washed clean and tender by the sea, like little shells. I put them in my mouth and she laughed and laughed. One year later she died of cancer. Twenty-three years old."

THE WINDOW with its bars receded before her, hiding in the sunshine, leaving only the chorus of cicadas. Lin Ying's body stiffened on the chair, then relaxed as she felt the moisture of her coming ooze between her fingers.

Lin Ying knew that when a man talked about the faults of another woman it was not all false, and when he talked about her better qualities it was not all true. But she had listened patiently, even with some interest. It was actually easier between them since they lacked any binding ties.

"Tell me, Jiangjiang, about the woman who used to ride your bike."

He held her against his chest and they shifted to lean against the wall together. "Same school, same department." He said that she looked a bit like Lin Ying, that they had been inseparable, did everything together. At first it was a joy, then it became a habit, and by the end it had turned into a rule that neither could break. "It became a duty I hated. It lasted seven full years. After we finished college, we were together again as graduate students. Both of us were exhausted. It only ended at graduation."

Lin Ying reached for the blanket and covered him. It is often cool in the middle of a Beijing summer night.

"The last time we saw each other was on an abandoned field. We walked toward each other, with this barbed-wire fence between us. We stood at the fence and yelled things. We both assumed that if the fence hadn't been there we would have tried to hit each other."

"I never thought of being together with you," Lin Ying said.

"Well, I've thought about it."

"When?" She touched his waist.

Li Jiangjiang tried to grab her hand but it was too late. She had already pulled back.

LIN YING'S face relaxed into a little smile. She picked up the cup on the table and held it between her hands, then drank half of the cooled water.

A curfew was now imposed every night. Guard posts were set up at every major intersection, the streets had soldiers patrolling, loaded rifles at the ready. News of the arrest of people on the wanted list had been coming in for the past week.

Lin Ying now loved nighttime more than ever before. Night hid much of the ugliness of day, and life also became simpler as night approached. Where will I be in June in the future? Will I be waiting and hoping for nightfall as I am now? Who will I be with then?

She thought no further. She didn't know how it would end with Li Jiangjiang, and she wasn't willing to push things to a conclusion or goal. Over a year ago, he had started the procedures to leave China to study in Germany in the autumn. He purposely did not raise the subject with her, and she didn't mention it either. The experience of 4 June had taught them one truth:

trying for something too hard often comes to nothing, and then you have spent your energy in vain.

Their emotional relationship was like making love in the ocean—perhaps in the next moment you would be knocked over by a wave, but you could also be lifted up to the crest.

3

She and the boy by the river had become good friends.

They grew up together, with pity for each other. When he was old enough to be sentenced to labor reform for stealing and was sent to work in a prison factory, she felt that she must act as though she were already married to him, devote all her love and fidelity to him. Her dreams were securely and sweetly confined to this infatuation.

"You're just like those women with their codes of honor whom I read about in novels when I was little." He said this to her when she came to visit him in jail, and her eyes filled with tears. Her tears before had all come from pain; now they were from happiness. Was she sacrificing herself to love? In fact, this kind of sacrifice was not so hard. All it took was winning the other person's respect and following a certain kind of moral code. Then, just as in the play when Wang Baochuan lives in a cave for eighteen years, honorably waiting for her husband, every moment of life has meaning and is fulfilled.

They agreed that they would marry when he got out of jail.

There were less than two years left, not even seven

hundred days. So far as she was concerned, the waiting was a kind of pleasure.

She sent him underwear, pen, ink, and paper. She visited him in jail once every two weeks. To her it was like a date. They saw each other in the prescribed time for visitors and could only hold each other's hands. I must work at reform as hard as I can, to be worthy of you, he would say earnestly, his eyes shining.

By then she was eighteen years old and working as an assistant bookkeeper in the wholesale factory outlet. All day long she flicked the balls on an abacus; sometimes the reported figures did not add up and she had to work on into the night. When her luck was bad it could be dawn before she went home. The dry, crisp clatter of the abacus was like the gurgle of a rippling stream to her, a pleasing sound. As she worked the abacus, she thought of him.

One spring morning she lifted her head to look out the window and suddenly saw him standing there, across the road, next to a stand that sold flat cakes. He must have been there awhile—perhaps hesitating to cross the road and come into the office. Catching sight of her now, he waved frantically.

She didn't believe her eyes, but yes, it was he. She threw down the account book and sped out the door, scrambled down the stairs, and plunged across the street to the other side, disregarding the honking cars. Right in front of everyone, she let him put his arm around her waist.

His shaved head looked comical shining in the sunlight there in the street. His clothes were clearly borrowed from someone else: far too large, hanging on his body. All the people in the street, all the people in her office stared at this strange couple.

She asked him how he had managed to get out of jail.

He pulled her into a small lane and told her that he missed her too much. In order to get out to see her, he had told the warden that on the outside he could manage to get some "scarce commodities" they needed. The labor-reform factory's production was being held up for lack of a particular kind of welding rod. The warden knew he was in love with a girl and wouldn't try to escape; he let him out for a few hours.

If he couldn't get the welding rods it would be bad news when he went back, the boy told her now. And he could forget about ever getting another leave. His voice was strained and pitiful.

She started making phone calls, contacting friends and colleagues, dashing all over the city, asking people to help. She made up stories to explain why she needed welding rods—she couldn't let him come with her or people would have been reluctant to help. When at last, panting, she put a heavy package of welding rods in his hands, there was only half an hour left before he was due back. He dashed for the bus.

She kept up her regular visits. He told her that books were not much use to him right now: his health wasn't good, there was too much work, the food was bad. So she brought honey, condensed milk, and other tasty but nutritious foods. Sometimes she would even buy him a pack of cigarettes. This was in the early eighties, when her salary, together with all the subsidies, came to fifty-five *yuan*. She spent half on him and gave her parents a portion of what was left. The remainder was just enough to pay for her own food.

A number of other men were attentive to her. She didn't even think about them. Her mother and father complained endlessly about her giving them too little: things were more and more expensive these days, a *yuan* wasn't worth what it used to be. When her father drank, his temper was as bad as ever, but he was older now and not healthy—he couldn't beat her but he could still give her looks. She didn't care. Other than crossing on the ferry to take her parents money, all her spare time was occupied with thoughts of love.

"I'll ask for another leave. Let's get married."

"Married?"

"What, you don't want to?" He was confused.

Marriage, she stammered, had to be certified by the work units of both man and woman. First you had to submit an application and get the approval of the department chief, then it was sent up a level, then another, for permission. The people wielding the "big seals" at her organization would never let her marry a convict doing labor reform, and without their certification it was hopeless, even if she went directly to the marriage registration office. Were the Party to find out, they would punish her. They would force her to tell everything, they might write up an investigation of her, and they might expel her. She lowered her head. She couldn't bear to say anything more.

"Then let's marry secretly!" He grabbed her hand.

She looked up at him and, without a moment's doubt, nodded in agreement. This did not require thought. It was the only rational, logical thing to do. This was love: romantic, steadfast, above vulgarity.

She collected the machinery parts he would need to take back with him. She put on a pink dress especially for him, thinking to herself that she looked like a bride, then waited for him out on the road. When he came, she furtively took him up to her room.

Her heart was pounding. She leaned against the tightly shut door, not daring to raise her blushing face. He came over to her slowly and, looking straight at her, gently stroked her face. Then he lifted her and laid her on the bed. He undid her dress roughly, ripping off the buttons, which fell to the floor.

"I'm still a virgin." Her entire being felt hot and trembled as she said it.

He kissed her, saying, "Of course. I know that. You're exactly as I've dreamed about night and day."

It was afternoon. The sunlight was glaring. The whistles of the steamships floated up from the river. Her tiny dormitory room was on the top floor, and in the heat of early summer it was scorching. Anxiously she watched as he took off his clothes. Sharp shadows from the intense light obscured his face but his ribs stood out clearly, and his torso was covered with scars as though he had been bitten all over by insects. Between his legs was a thing that terrified her, that, almost like an electric shock, made her close her eyes. Her breath stopped in her throat. She felt dizzy.

His body pressed heavily down on hers. He ground against her, turning sideways from time to time to manipulate himself, then pressing down on her again. His hands groped around her body; his face dripped with sweat.

She had no idea how to help him. Then suddenly came a sharp ripping pain from her vagina. Moaning, she opened her eyes just at the moment that he retreated. He held up fingers dripping with blood. He looked at the blood, transfixed.

"You really are a virgin." A smile of contentment passed across his face.

"You . . . why did you use your fingers?" she said, trying hard not to cry.

"Because now you belong to me." He said it matter-of-factly, as though this was not an issue for discussion.

She climbed off the bed, slowly picked up the pink dress flung on the floor, and put it on.

Suddenly he kneeled before her and buried his face in his hands. "Please forgive me, I beg you, I beg you. You don't know what the men in prison can be like." He was crying.

Her mind was completely blank. She continued dressing, putting on her plastic sandals.

"Why don't you ask me? All right, I'll tell you anyway." His wailing suddenly stopped. He stood up again and his body was shaking as he yelled, "It's not a place for human beings! Neither your mind nor your body belongs to you. I took it too much . . . In the end, I wanted to do it myself! But I can't satisfy you like a real man!"

"I was completely willing to wait for you, wait until you got out of jail." She retreated in horror to the bed now and tears started flowing. "How could you have thought of doing such a thing to me?"

He sat down heavily. "I couldn't stand to have you marry anyone else," he said hoarsely. His pitifulness was harder to take than his roughness earlier.

She understood him completely. Even if she'd been stupider, she still wouldn't have missed the meaning.

No man would marry her now—and even if one did, she'd be a scorned woman, for she was no longer a virgin. Wronged, humiliated. How could she have been such an idiot as to entrust her whole life to this person? The childish fairy tale that she had constructed had been ripped asunder, broken with a few fingers. Each drop of red mocked her.

She pulled out her package, wrapped in brown paper and tied with string, from under the bed and handed it to him. She told him to go.

"You'll regret this! You'll come looking for me, begging me!" His every word was vehement.

The door slammed and his stomping footsteps were soon gone. The sun seemed to be suspended in the center of the window, abnormally orange, and the light seemed to come in pulses, now long, now short. She turned on the water and washed her face, itching and flushed from tears. When they started up again, she turned on the shower, pointed the water straight on her body, and let it run down her clothes.

Dusk was approaching. She thought of catching the ferry to her parents' house. It was already the time of day when lamps are lit—on the river and over on the other bank she could see patches of light in the darkness. There weren't many people on the ferry, and it reached the other side quickly. But she did not really want to see her family. Even less did she want to walk along the gravel beach where she and he had played together as children. She took the same ferry back to her own side. Turning on the lamp in her room, she sat down to write. She was accustomed to keeping a diary, but this evening the words on the paper were disjointed. The diary was too small; there wasn't enough space to write all she had to say. She threw it aside and took a blank piece of paper from the drawer.

The minute she started to write a poem, she felt like a different person.

> In the hidden shadow of my past
> is set aside an icy skull
> of a convict I used to love.

> No more time to discuss it now.
> I've always loved those I shouldn't,
> or perhaps I should say, I've always forgiven them.

Several years later she read this poem aloud to an audience—by the ocean, at a Beibuwan poetry gathering. Familiar faces flickered, but they were those of strangers. His face seemed to be among them. "Do you still hate me?" he seemed to be asking.

She smiled. Her poem had answered for her long ago.

> It was you who taught me to become the worst kind of
>   woman.
> You said that women must be like that.
> The rose I pinned on you
> Could be my future, could be this one evening,
> Could be constantly changing lips
> Or the whole world.

> What I want is for this whole world to become a sheet of
>   blackness
> That can be rolled up
> The way this century's tears
> Have been collected in my pupils.

The telephone had rung in her hotel room after the reading. Lin Ying had picked up the receiver and heard a voice say, "What kind of poetry was that? Incantations of some kind of shaman!"

It was a literary critic considerably older than she was, someone who had declared himself her mentor. He was trying to express his concern. In a newspaper interview, he had said that the Party's policies on literary matters had not changed: let one hundred flowers bloom, one hundred schools of thought contend. We welcome all styles of poetry. We have, please note, invited several so-called underground poets to this conference, for example, Comrade Lin Ying. He had mentioned several famous poets who had already received government prizes and forecast that Lin Ying and others would soon join their ranks.

Lin Ying understood why he was upset. Not only should she not write this kind of decadent, pessimistic poetry, but she surely shouldn't recite it at this kind of public event. She had let him down, dashed his hopes for her. Her hotel room was on the second floor. Sitting with her were two local underground poets and a young literary critic who was interested in her poetry, Li Jiang-jiang, who had come from Beijing.

Lin Ying understood the man on the line, but suddenly she felt her temper rising. She shouted into the telephone: "That's exactly what my poems are—incantations of a shaman!"

Hearing her tone, the man on the end of the receiver laughed. He said, "Come to my room in a little while, why don't you? Room 405."

"Of course I should love to pay my respects," Lin Ying said calmly, turning the tables on him. "I look forward to your esteemed advice tomorrow at the conference." She heard the receiver on the other end slam down.

She hung up, was silent for a moment. In the short time she had been a writer she had managed to alienate quite a few people by not accepting this kind of arrangement—call it advice, instruction, entreaty. She had quite clearly understood his intent, exactly what he was hoping for. However, she not only did not accept the favor but left no room for a graceful retreat. She had never been smooth or slick in social relations. She could not do things in the acceptable way. Moreover, she was fundamentally uninterested in doing anything in the acceptable way.

4

For eleven days there had been no news of Chen Yu. Whenever the telephone rang in the hall, Lin Ying's heart missed a beat. She had to keep herself from running out to pick it up.

Once someone in the corridor shouted, "Lin Ying, telephone!" When she dashed out to take the receiver and said hello, there was no response. She said it again, but the other person hung up.

It must have been Chen Yu. Her eyes misted over. She leaned against the wall to calm herself for a moment, then dialed Chen Yu's number. No answer. She dialed again, this time his office. Someone answered and said Chen Yu wasn't there. Had he come to work? No, the person said, he hadn't come to work.

"For how long?" she persisted.

The impatient answer came, "A week!" Then the person hung up.

Dejected, she returned to her room. She didn't care what kind of news it was—any news would be better than none. But why do I need news of Chen Yu?

LI JIANGJIANG came back from work in a bad mood. The propaganda department of the Central Committee had sent a group to occupy the Art Institute and other cultural organizations. Everyone had to be tried, to explain what he had been doing before and after 4 June. What meetings attended? What speeches given? What petitions signed? What demonstrations attended? What slogans shouted? Who is there to vouch for you? Party members who had publicly withdrawn from the Party had to go further and "hand over," or accuse, those whom they considered "instigators." Everyone was informing on everyone else. Any behavior since the beginning of the "capitalist-class liberalization" of the early 1980s was open to question.

The atmosphere in the institute was very tense, Li Jiangjiang reported. People were doubting each other, were pushing the blame onto others. In an article written earlier in the year for the *Review of Chinese and Foreign Literature*, he had used a psychoanalytic approach to interpret the erotic seventeenth-century novel *Golden Lotus*. His article had now been criticized by the newly appointed director sent by the propaganda department. It was considered as being "outrageous," Li Jiangjiang snorted. The new director even put into his report on Li Jiangjiang that he had not realized how low the morals of this batch of young "critics" had fallen.

" 'A decline in morals necessarily leads to a decline in political consciousness,' is what he said." Li Jiangjiang paced angrily around the room.

"He has a pretty good eye." Lin Ying sighed.

A fly buzzed at the window, trying to escape from the room. The netting over the window, fixed tightly to the frame, mercilessly blocked its way.

Li Jiangjiang talked about various matters at the institute, but he didn't ask how Lin Ying had passed her day. He knew nothing at all about Lin Ying's parents, her sisters, her past life, and he showed no interest in knowing about them. Naturally, Lin Ying was not willing to bring any of this up. The two of them carried dinner back from the canteen every night. The cooks were trying to feed the young people living there as well as they could—they'd add more choices, and the portions were generous and cheap. Normally if you rubbed them the wrong way they got angry, but now they were uncommonly patient and civil. "Just tell us what you want to eat. We'll make it for you. The old ones said it best, 'So long as the mountains stay green, you won't have to worry about firewood.' "

Li Jiangjiang gave Lin Ying all the beef in his bowl. He faced the wall and sat mute, chopsticks in his hand, not moving. "Don't get upset about those rotten stinking pickles, those self-styled Marxist theoreticians," she said to him. "Right now, the more you argue the facts with them, the more you play into their hands."

It was cooler in the evening. They lay on the narrow bed, Lin Ying's slender body on one side, giving more than half the space to him. The clean fragrance of the straw mattress wafted through the air.

A cool fog moved up from the surface of the water, climbing the riverbank, passing through flimsy doors, penetrating rooms, until one could see nothing near or far and the ground slowly disappeared. She moved toward a flurry of sound behind her. Two walls locked her into a dead end where two open sewers flowed together. Someone sat there alone, anxiously washing a large basin of dirty clothes. "Never finished no matter how I wash. The more I wash, the more there are!" From the sewers came a horribly foul odor. She wanted to cover her nose but didn't know where her hand was. Nearby a wooden double door screeched as it blew back and forth in the wind, as though it might fall on her at any moment. She retreated backward into the thick mist. As she took her last look, the person's silhouette seemed from the rear like her father's.

Without waking, she knew she was in a dream.

She walked toward a bus parked at the side of a street. Just as she got on the bus it started moving forward, picked up speed, then began careening down the road, rolling ever faster down a steep slope. She gripped the handrail above her and shouted, "Stop the bus!" Instead, the bus continued plunging wildly down the mountain. She could see her swaying body in the rear-view mirror, but she couldn't move or make a sound when she discovered, terrified, that there was no driver in the driver's seat. All the passengers were shouting now. No one knew what to do. At last she grabbed the steering wheel but it wouldn't move, so she let go and the bus went on rolling down the mountain.

She opened her eyes. Li Jiangjiang was sitting by the lamp without a shirt on. Lin Ying asked why he wasn't asleep. He showed her what he was reading—an old book on the metaphysics of speculation.

"The leadership urges you to read more Marxism and Leninism. What are you doing with this feudalist stuff?"

"I don't need the feudalist class to do my thinking for me." Li Jiangjiang put the book down and sat beside her. "I'm just reading to find out why others are so wrong and I'm so right."

"You're a brazen braggart." She pulled her knees in and sat up, tossing the flowered bedspread over him. It hung from his head all the way to the floor. "Let's see if Chinese dream interpretation is better than Freud's."

Li Jiangjiang stood up and staggered dramatically back and forth, his shadow on the wall mounting from very small to enormous.

"Of course it is! What did you dream just now? Tell me—I'm sure I can interpret it."

"My dream just now wasn't so bad," she said. "At least it was a lot less bloody than others recently. But never mind my current dreams—they're too real."

"Then tell me some dream you've had before. The most interesting one."

"Dreams are strange." Lin Ying stared at Li Jiang-jiang's shadow on the wall. "More often than not, mine have been like premonitions. I've often felt that a place I've never been to, people I've never met I've somehow seen before. Thinking back, I realize I've seen them in dreams."

"That's altogether possible. Quick, tell me a specific dream!" He was impatient.

"I dreamed I saw a fish, a nice big one, its scales flashing. It was swishing its tail, scattering seed in the depths of the water, like rain. What do you think that means?" she asked, deadpan.

Li Jiangjiang tilted his head back and the bedspread fell off; with one jump, he landed on the bed, pulling her down with him. "What an obscene dream. The fat fish is me. I'm a big carp. And I can scatter seed in the deepest depths."

"You're shameless, aren't you? Listen to that, so superficial. And here you are making fun of Freud and Marx. You think you aren't a decadent writer?" She caressed his hair. "Last night I dreamed I saw someone but couldn't tell who he was. His face was obscured by a smile."

"Couldn't have been me. You may not want my love, but you'll never not be able to see me clearly."

Lin Ying felt that the man who said this was a child, even though Li Jiangjiang was not just a grown man but sometimes so tyrannical it moved her.

She had been making forty-two *yuan* at the factory. Various supplements for housing and other things brought the total to sixty-five *yuan*. This she had sacrificed when she started studying, even though she still nominally kept the job. There hadn't been a problem before. Every province and city government paid salaries to poets who were designated professionals, whether they wrote a word or not. And although she didn't have the luck to be included among them, there were countless newspapers and magazines in China, and even a small county newspaper paid a fee for what they published—the standard amount was ten *yuan* for twenty lines of poetry. If you published several poems a month you could earn more than the official salary.

However, many works that had been accepted by publications were now being rejected. If you wanted to publish, you had to write something in the "realism" vein that applauded the Communist Party. Or you could avoid reality entirely and indulge in folksy sentimentality, and the simpler and more transparent the writing the better. One couldn't put in any "avant-garde" twists and turns, and certainly not a drop of the dark rain of individualism.

Lin Ying was not willing to be this kind of white-washed poet, and so her income dropped. Li Jiangjiang said his salary was enough for both of them—other than eating, all they had to pay for was toothpaste, detergent, and a few other little things. He was unwilling to accept any of the money that Lin Ying got from her little sister. "Hold on to it—it may come in handy sometime." Lin Ying disagreed, saying she ought at least pay for her food coupons. "Well then, let's say that for now I'm loaning the money to you." He got angry. "Keep this up and I'll be unhappy." Didn't he realize that she would be even more unhappy?

Right now, as Lin Ying was daydreaming, he already had his underpants off and had pulled the covers back. His body slipped into hers.

"It would be better if we'd never got to know each other."

"Why?"

"I'd come quicker."

She rolled over on top of him. Her hair covered his face. Riding and being ridden were certainly different.

"But I don't like it fast," he mumbled.

"What you don't like is women taking the initiative, right?"

Li Jiangjiang said something. Lin Ying moved, and at a crucial moment got a bite, just one bite, and she no longer heard what he was saying. Her eyes were shut tight, she forgot where she was, her entire body shook, until a dizzy ecstasy bore into her inner depths, pressing her down.

The sky was getting light now by five in the morning.

Li Jiangjiang was sound asleep when Lin Ying quietly left the bed. She went to the window. For some reason she had wakened too easily. Outside the curtains was a hazy sky, below the window was a playing field with two white poplars and some bushes. She put on her clothes, opened the door and went downstairs. Under the tall poplars the dawn was especially cool. She crossed her arms over her chest. It was quiet—no birds, no chirping of crickets yet. The few cars that passed every minute or so made scarcely any noise.

Too calm. Too calm wasn't good. It always forced her back to the old subject.

5

Then, too, the crickets called endlessly, summer after summer.

Year upon year, the things that came together to form their lives were a post office, a train, a little hotel, a telephone, and letters—most importantly, letters. She scarcely ever had to read either his letters or her own a second time before they were engraved in her memory.

. . . Nobody knows the truth of why we went into hiding. It was only an accident in the snow, as I saw the bushes turn from purple to blue. It is destined that we shall meet again at that bright spot in the scenery.

. . . You painted images on my body. With every move the garden you made swells and grows.

. . . Love has favored us and will not let go. This love is being soaked through in the storm outside. It struggles, calls, falls down, then rises calmly and walks toward our door.

. . . Hands are covering my hands, forming an eye of desperation.

. . . I have a seat for you. We seem to be sitting together. A few pretty wings flash across the window. Where from? Seven days. I have been missing for seven whole days.

Train-station platform. Train. Platform.

Several years passed in a moment. Wheels rolled along the tracks, keeping time to the shrill call of the melancholy whistle. When she was most solitary, most alone, she realized she was silently reciting his letters.

It was Chen Yu who first discovered Lin Ying's poetry. He'd gone to her mountain city on a business trip, and the editor of the local magazine went to his hotel to pay a call on this person from the Central News Agency. He brought a pile of publications to let him get a sense of the place; when Chen Yu read Lin Ying's poetry he was amazed that such a provincial backwater would have a writer of such style and refinement. He asked for the address of this unrecognized poet, and when he returned to Beijing, he sent Lin Ying a letter.

From the start, their emotions were urgent. Chen Yu had a wife, a college classmate who now worked in a publishing house. Chen Yu said that even if he had not met Lin Ying, he and Mei Ling would be taking different roads. If he didn't bring up divorce, she would. He took every opportunity he had to come on business to the mountain city, and when his excuses ran out, he got Lin Ying to ask for leave to come to Beijing. Several times he tried to get her transferred but never succeeded. Each short time together was followed by a long period of separation.

"Yu, it'd be better to die, get it over with. At least that way we'd be together. Living like this is too painful."

"You're right. It really is too painful."

Once this was said, she felt better.

Chen Yu was always comforting her. "We won't have to live like this for long." Still, the divorce proceedings were taking a long time. Perhaps out of pride, perhaps out of trust in him, Lin Ying didn't push, but privately she worried.

"Why didn't I meet you earlier—that way I wouldn't have fallen into her hands." Chen Yu and Mei Ling had already begun living apart, he said, and as soon as the divorce went through he would marry Lin Ying.

Naturally Lin Ying took statements like this as proof of his love. Her better judgment told her she shouldn't place her fate in the hands of another person, but love was a dazzling rainbow in her otherwise dingy world.

She declared herself a poet. Writing excellent poetry was the main aim in her life.

Chen Yu wrote back that he very much appreciated this in her, that this was what made him love her so madly.

Chen Yu was a man of ambition. The newspaper he

worked for employed close to ten thousand people—there was no other newspaper like it in the world. In such a place, to be promoted was harder than for one of the three thousand beauties of the harem palace to be selected for the emperor's favors. But Chen Yu was promoted. He rose and rose in the late 1980s, when the reform faction of the Communist Party had achieved a degree of power. Some said Chen Yu was already considered part of a certain brain trust. He denied it. Lin Ying wasn't interested in his official position, anyway, and never asked him for details.

But finally her chance came. She passed the exam for the writing program at the Beijing Normal University; it had been very hard work and it had its price but she felt it was worth it. She had tried to shut herself off from slander and local gossip. Beyond going to work every day, she stayed at home, behind closed doors, holding out for the long-awaited time when she could leave this closed-minded provincial town for Beijing. Her pounding heart kept telling her, This time you will truly spread your wings and fly.

She made a long-distance call to Beijing and told Chen Yu the good news. He seemed shocked for a moment, speechless. Lin Ying began to have doubts: perhaps he'd been struck dumb not from excitement but from worry about her coming to Beijing?

The train pulled into the Beijing railway station. The railway car slowly emptied and the platform filled with people. Lin Ying looked out the window, not daring to hope. But there was Chen Yu, standing near the exit, not moving, letting the passengers and the people greeting them flow around him. The way he stood there made Lin Ying feel that he'd been waiting for days, years, lifetimes, that his body was exhausted but his eyes flashed with fire. Her last shred of doubt disappeared and she felt ashamed of herself.

Mei Ling lived in a different dormitory. Lin Ying never saw her in person but saw her photograph and could tell that she was an elegant woman. Her eyes weren't big but they sparkled, and her face was lightly freckled—a classic southern beauty. In fact, it was hard to put the inferior piece of goods that Chen Yu described together with the image in the photograph.

Only when she got to Beijing did Lin Ying learn that the reason the divorce was going so slowly was that Chen Yu insisted on settling it out of court, since both husband and wife were relatively high in their units and both needed to maintain their good reputations. Going to court would tarnish their image. Mei Ling, of course, could use Chen Yu's aversion to bad publicity to drag out the proceedings.

Chen Yu had watched Lin Ying, thinner than ever, walk to the window and stare out at the snowflakes filling the air. Sitting on the couch, he had vowed to conclude the divorce process as soon as possible. Lin Ying had the feeling that there was something wrong in all this somewhere, that her life might be built on air.

But then, all too quickly, came that spring when heaven and earth turned upside down. Everything personal or individual became secondary or completely irrelevant. Without hesitation, Lin Ying plunged ahead.

6

The hall telephone rang. Nobody picked it up. On the tenth ring, something snapped inside her and she sprinted for the corridor.

"Little Ying, it's me." Chen Yu's voice was soft and gentle, as though nothing had happened between them, as though everything was as it had been and no explanation was necessary.

Lin Ying also feigned indifference. "What's up?"

Chen Yu told her he'd like her to come home, even just once.

Lin Ying could not keep it up. "Don't forget, you're a man with a wife."

Chen Yu said slowly, patiently, "I'm a man in the process of getting a divorce, and what's more, it's on account of you that I've made this decision, that I am working so hard on it. I'll tell you frankly, that night Mei Ling came fleeing from Nanchizikou, right on the Avenue of Eternal Peace. She rode her bike to my place, weeping. I could see she'd had a great shock. I had to comfort her, and so she stayed over."

Without intending to, Lin Ying let out a sigh. That one short night, everything that should never have happened did happen. She, too, had been at the square and she should sympathize with Mei Ling. But the things she had seen had gutted her of feelings, ripped away any trust she had in people. The way Chen Yu's head had turned involuntarily to the side, toward the bed, the way his hand had slid out from underneath Mei Ling's body—she had replayed this countless times in her mind; it had become a fixation. Every posture, every movement that she and Chen Yu enjoyed in their love-making had doubtless been repeated by Mei Ling too, just as at the beginning she herself had repeated what Mei Ling did.

She laughed coldly. "Stayed over! Mr. Editor in Chief, you really know how to pick your words. Why don't you just say right out what you were doing?"

She suddenly sensed that Mei Ling had always meant her to see the two of them in bed one day. When a marriage falls apart, the husband and wife can agree on terms and part amicably if the husband isn't seeing anyone else. A wife can even cast a man off with the greatest of ease, a carefree gesture—fine, we each go our own way. But if the husband is seeing someone else, what was simple becomes far more complex. And if a wife believes that the enemy is worthy of her competition, she will devise any means on earth to win.

The more Lin Ying thought about this the more distraught she became. She was scarcely aware of the voice on the other end of the line.

"I'll say it again. Please forgive me. Come back, just one time!" Chen Yu sounded utterly sincere.

Something up her nose pinched, and she instantly wanted to respond to his plea, but her reason refused. He's a faker! Don't accept! Don't be a weak female!

"Well," she finally answered, "I'll speak frankly to you, too. I know perfectly well what position I'm in. I'm a third wheel." She didn't care about her status, but she couldn't bear his not speaking the truth, not admitting that he was in between a wife and a mistress, his life intimately connected to both, and that in wavering, unresolved, between them, he was injuring not just them but his own integrity.

There was a long silence. The wire clearly transmitted the uneven sound of his breathing as though he was reflecting hard on something. Lin Ying waited patiently until finally his voice came through. "You may not realize my position. But it's not possible for me to deal with these things right now."

"Ha, regrets. Eat your words. You're not willing to risk your position at the height of your career. Well, I wish you success in mending the broken mirror." She slammed down the receiver, not wanting to hear his voice again.

Hua Hua appeared by the stairs and saw her standing there, motionless, hand pressed against the wall, head down. Without saying a word, she came down and hugged Lin Ying. They pressed their heads together.

She followed Hua Hua down the stairs. "Fate is never kind to women poets," the actress said.

"It's nothing," murmured Lin Ying. "Fortune and happiness don't suit me. I couldn't have them if I wanted, and anyway, I don't care." The goddess of poetry must surely have a garbage pail, she thought. Without even looking you could be certain that it was mostly filled with the whitened bones of tearful women.

Hua Hua told her she had written a few poems in college but fortunately had not continued. "This must be one of the loneliest times of all for a poet." She pushed opened the door to the courtyard. "Lin Ying, what you must do is harden your heart."

By four or five o'clock, the sun was hidden in the evening haze, and a soft glow was cast on the courtyard eaves and walls. The two women took a shortcut past the flower garden.

The more she considered it, the more Lin Ying felt she had been immeasurably stupid. She and Chen Yu had even argued over who loved the other more. It was hard to believe, but they really had—half in earnest, half in jest. Lin Ying had said, "I win. The way you stroke me is in a straight line, never in a circle."

Chen Yu had said, "No, I win. You make love in the day and write at night. Whereas my nights belong completely to you. I don't hold anything back for myself."

"I win. When I was in the mountain city, if I didn't get a letter from you every day I'd stop eating and not be able to sleep."

"I win. If I went a day in Beijing without a letter from you, I'd have to masturbate."

"A lie!" Lin Ying had shouted. "I've never seen you masturbate in your life. You're a cold-blooded animal."

Lin Ying blushed to think about it. It wasn't that the pillow talk had been so intimate but that she had been so naive as to have been moved by it, to have taken it as the expression of true feelings.

She and Hua Hua walked around the courtyard, then went out through a small wooden gate by the canteen. They crossed the road and came to shops along one side of a street—restaurants, key makers, shoe repairmen, and a pitiful little theater advertising a kung fu movie from Hong Kong. In the distance were several hotels but there were no guests in sight and very few cars parked in front.

"All love loves to do is play around with women," Hua Hua said.

Lin Ying went past the woman selling ice pops.

"Isn't it just because this bag of a body is filled with all kinds of odd bits and pieces—isn't that why it's so painful?"

They stopped at a fruit stand. Lin Ying bought a muskmelon and asked the person at the stand for a knife. Gritting her teeth, she fiercely stabbed the melon and split it in two. She gave half to Hua Hua.

7

Lin Ying sat on the side of the bed, listlessly picking up the newspapers that Li Jiangjiang had brought back. He had turned on a light, even though the curtain of evening had not yet been completely drawn over the sky.

"Just read to see what's going on. Don't take it to heart," Li Jiangjiang said as he played with the radio dial.

Spread before her were photographs and articles about how the highest leaders in the land were saluting the troops who had come to Beijing to enforce martial law. The entire country was once again united in harmony and peace, they were asserting. Lin Ying threw the paper aside and pulled a different one from the middle of the stack. Bold headlines sprang out: EMERGENCY NOTIFICATION OF MUNICIPAL GOVERNMENT AND MARTIAL LAW TROOPS. Her hand shrank back. The paper slipped to the bed, then settled comfortably on the hard cement floor. "Antirevolutionary rioting . . . thugs . . . burning, smashing, looting . . ."

"What are you doing bringing these things back here?" she asked. "They're plastered all over the streets!"

"They flew off the wall and landed on my bicycle."

Li Jiangjiang left the radio and came over to her. After restacking the papers on the bed he bent over and picked up the emergency notification. "One day it will be fun to see this." He folded it into a small square and stuck it in the lowest shelf of the bookcase.

But then he said, as he straightened up, "Well, in whichever life we're living, we won't find fun." And he kneeled again to pull out the notice. His movement was too rough, and books came tumbling out on the floor. All clumsiness, he tried to hold the books back and at the same time pull the notice out from underneath— one yank and it ripped in two. He threw the pieces in the direction of the wastepaper basket, but one fell on the floor. Lin Ying leaned over to pick it up and saw the words she did not want to see: "Severely punish . . . those who harbor criminals . . . inform against offenders . . . large rewards . . ."

"Every persecution movement that the Communist Party has begun ends with a 'correction,' with a sly semiadmission of an error. Then they try to rehabilitate those who were hurt," she said.

"Don't be so optimistic," Li Jiangjiang replied. "Rehabilitation will take ten years, twenty, thirty . . . If one were really patient one could wait a lifetime." He began playing with the radio dial again.

". . . Senate . . . condemns . . . economic sanctions . . ."

Lin Ying's gaze moved to the landscape on the wall, the snow-white Himalayas rising range after range, a boundless horizon without human problems, with none of the disasters brought on by mankind, no slogans, no banners, certainly no terror, no hatred. Earlier in the spring, if she didn't go to the square for a day she felt uneasy, as though only in a crowd of shouting people could life have meaning. It was so simple: with one goal reached, every other problem would be resolved.

For the first time, she began to doubt whether her actions that spring had been right.

"Theorizing and creating are quite different," Li Jiangjiang said pointedly. He turned off the radio and stood up. "Theory requires clarity and definition, transparency. Creativity requires vagueness, indistinctness, and often lingers on the surface."

"Are you saying I'm superficial?" Lin Ying approached him. "Are you even saying I should be content with being skin-deep?"

Li Jiangjiang put his hand on her bare arm, below her short-sleeved shirt. "That's plenty deep enough when you have skin like this."

Her skin rippled like water from his touch.

She felt she had fallen into a strange realm: fleeing with all her might, she hung now from a withered vine, suspended over an abyss. Above and below were wolves, bloody fangs bared, anticipating. Two small mice were slowly gnawing through the vine: her doom was a matter of minutes at most. But just then she discovered beautiful fresh strawberries within reaching distance. Should she pluck them and toss them into her mouth?

She could always think of this moment as happening in some other, different summer. Tonight was serene and auspicious, unique. And when yet another white dawn had disappeared, a school of shining fish would again be swimming toward the depths of the ocean.

She held him, her eyes half closed, her lips moist and red. He slipped out of her arms and knelt on one knee.

Lifting her skirt he kissed her knees, her thighs, then pressed his head against her soft triangular mound. His hands clasped hers. Azure waves throbbed with an irregular beat. The two of them felt cast into space by a celestial swing.

When the door opened they both heard the sound but did not respond. Their movements, as if in slow motion, drew them out of their own world. Hands loosened and opened, they slowly turned to face the door and only then saw Chen Yu standing there.

8

He walked in from the darkness of the corridor. He was dressed formally, as though he had come to do official business. His face was fresh-shaven, so that he looked slightly pale. He stopped by the wooden chair between the door and the bookshelf, then sat down. He wasn't grim or angry; he looked calm. His eyes did not waver but his hand reached into his pocket for a cigarette. He flicked a lighter twice, then began to smoke.

Li Jiangjiang scrambled up from his kneeling position. Lin Ying quickly pulled down her skirt and smoothed her blouse, then stood paralyzed.

Chen Yu said casually, "As I thought. Shameless."

Li Jiangjiang took a step forward. "Don't insult me." His face was bright red.

"I didn't mean you." Chen Yu blew a puff of smoke and turned to Li Jiangjiang, slowly drawling the words. He continued to smoke. "But now that I think of it, when I telephoned to ask you to go past the Yellow Temple and Balipu to find Lin Ying and look after her, I wasn't asking you to take care of her in bed."

Lin Ying was too shocked to speak. Had Chen Yu arranged it all? How could she have not thought of this—why, on the morning of the fourth, on a street of panic and terror, had she just happened to meet up with Li Jiangjiang? In the end she had never escaped from the palm Chen Yu's hand.

"You have no right." Li Jiangjiang was burning with anger. "You have no right to order me or Lin Ying about. She's an independent person."

Chen Yu paid no attention. He said to Lin Ying now, "You really can organize a coincidence, can you? You thought I would be as jealous as you are? You're wrong. I'm not able to hang on to something endlessly like that."

Furious, Lin Ying felt that her skull was going to split apart. She had never imagined that Chen Yu could be so diabolical, rationalizing things as it suited him, not letting her say a word. She stared at him. This casual smoking pose was particularly nasty. "You're the most despicable man I've ever met," she said.

Chen Yu stood up and came closer. "Don't be so sure." He pointed at Li Jiangjiang. "I'd bet this man is no better than I am in any respect."

"Who do you think you are?" Li Jiangjiang brandished his fist as though ready to fight. But instead of charging Chen Yu, he stomped to the door and pulled it open. "Get out. I'm telling you, you fucker, get out!"

Chen Yu gave him a spiteful look. The two men were the same height and Chen Yu was not much older, though he was more solid and acted more experienced and mature. As he moved to the door, he threw down his cigarette and ground it out with his heel.

"Lin Ying, our relationship ends here. Don't come

looking for me after this." Then, to Li Jiangjiang, whose furious face glistened with sweat, "That goes for our relationship too. You're no friend of mine."

Chen Yu strode out the door. In less than two seconds he was back, paying no attention to Li Jiangjiang, who was about to yell again. He looked at Lin Ying and pointed behind the door. "Just to let you know, I brought you your things."

Lin Ying and Li Jiangjiang were stunned. Chen Yu's face was as emotionless as it had been when he had first come in. Lin Ying could not believe that this was the man she had known. Letters floated down from the sky to obliterate his face.

She felt supremely ashamed of herself, ashamed that her life had been so manipulated by men. Chen Yu had not come to take her back. Instead, he was throwing her away as he might a used battery. And she had given the bastard a convenient moral excuse. She could imagine how pleased he must be as he walked out the door.

She chased him down the corridor, hoping to catch up and shout a few things at his back to relieve her anger, but the sound of his footsteps had already vanished. The dark corridor was empty. From behind the other doors came the muffled clamor of televisions and radios. Furious, she gave the door of Li Jiangjiang's room a kick. It squeaked back and forth as if wronged.

"How can he go abusing people like that?" Li Jiangjiang's voice was not raised but it cut clearly through the air.

All by herself, Lin Ying pushed her bag from the hall into the room, slamming the door shut with her back. It was her only bag, a black suitcase with wheels. She knelt to wipe off the dust on it—and the man's fingerprints in the dust. She rubbed vigorously, over and over. Li Jiangjiang paced back and forth behind her, gesticulating, cursing. Perhaps he had never come to blows like this with anyone before and wasn't used to fighting with words.

The air was hot and heavy. Crickets had been calling all afternoon and were still ardently declaring their delight in heaven and earth. Lin Ying wiped her face with her hands; sweat or tears had made channels through the dirt on her cheeks. She was as helpless as a child, as though she had returned to the riverside and was balancing a heavy load of sand, facing the endless stone steps, trying to keep moving without even the strength to cry.

9

A crack in the sky opened into a gaping hole, issuing forth blood and fire. Gong Gong, the male god, had burst it open with his head in the heat of a struggle for power. Nu Wo, the female god, ancestor of we women, finally patched the sky back together again, despite the searing pain. Why is it that from the ancient past until today, whenever things go wrong, it's always women who have to put it right?

Hua Hua opened her door and greeted Lin Ying happily. "Welcome! How does the great poet find time to honor us with a visit!"

Shao Liuliu's exaggerated voice added from inside the room, "So the celestial maiden descends to the earthly realm—wonder what heavenly laws she's been breaking!"

The room was lit only by a table lamp and the window was open. The two women were smoking and drinking beer, but instead of smoke and alcohol there was a faint scent of jasmine in the air. "Have I come at the wrong time?" Lin Ying asked. She had only wanted to visit for a while with Hua Hua, to ease her mind.

"Not at all!" The two of them said she needn't act like a stranger just because she hadn't seen them for a few days.

"I'm not in a good mood," Lin Ying said. She stood before the lamp, her shadow large on the wall.

Shao Liuliu covered her face with her hand and said, in mock seriousness, "My mood's not too good either."

Hua Hua flicked her cigarette ashes and drawled, "In a year like this, whose is?"

Lin Ying hung her head. "I'm not talking about world affairs or national events. I can't get over my own problems."

"True, in times like this we women take the brunt of it." Hua Hua sat Lin Ying on a chair, took out a glass, and poured her some beer.

She stood by the chair, her hair hanging straight to her shoulders, a dark-green skirt outlining the contours of her tall, graceful body. "We women," she said, "we're the showcase of this masculine world. All men have ever given women is tiny bound feet and a contract to buy their bodies. When we could have gotten an official cap or a mortarboard. Women are just a tool for carrying on the male lineage, to bear its progeny as they always have."

"I wish time could go back a few centuries! The best would be to the world of the *Strange Tales of Liao Zhai*. Those fox spirits dared to cry, complain, curse—

they all had emotions, desires, and they were braver than any man." Shao Liuliu was vehement. "Not one man today would dare love a fox spirit."

"Too true." Hua Hua smoked elegantly, rings puffing from her moist red lips. "Men divide women into three types: wives, witches, and whores. The tiring work goes to wives, the evil work goes to witches, the dirty work goes to whores—only the men are allowed to be great and wise."

Lin Ying smiled. No wonder the artsy circles in Beijing called her Hua Hua the Irresistible. Her wit was sharp and she showed no mercy toward the male sex.

Hua Hua went to the table at the foot of the bed and pulled open the drawer. "We're not in a good mood, so how about watching some videos for women. How about it?"

Shao Liuliu sipped her beer. "Yellow. Only yellow. Only off-color." She was fashionably turned out from head to toe—a tight denim skirt, a black cotton shirt that showed her shoulders and clung to her body, a bright gold necklace. Nobody could believe that she was a classical musician, her music the refined purity of the lute. Lin Ying had admired her virtuosity when she heard her perform the *Prelude to Peach-Blossom Fan*.

Shao Liuliu started talking about how her husband was beginning to doubt if his daughter was really his; he was always looking for trouble in that regard. "I told him to take her for a blood test, but he wouldn't go. 'Scared to.' I asked him what he was scared of. 'Scared of the truth.' I told him he had some kind of mental illness, he was so jealous."

Hua Hua put on a video. "Let's watch this one first. Seems a little more refined. Liuliu, it seems to me you should get rid of that man of yours as soon as possible. Have pity on him—don't bully him to death."

The screen flickered with shadows and words, and then two hunks, Western men, could be seen, one on the telephone, the other hurriedly straightening up the room, both with towels wrapped around their waists. Most of the floor was covered in Japanese-style tatami, nice and spacious, and the blinds were pulled up—skyscrapers could be seen outside and sunshine poured into the room.

In the next scene, a luxury sedan pulled up to the front door of a hotel. A young woman in a leopard-skin coat was sitting in the back, and her movements as she got out were aristocratic and dignified. She came into the room and bestowed a condescending kiss on each of the two men, then took off her coat. Underneath she was wearing a black negligee. She threw the coat to the man who had been on the telephone, and he took it respectfully while the other man gestured politely toward the bed.

Shao Liuliu clapped her hands and shrieked, "I've seen this one before. It's called *Male Prostitutes*. It's almost too much, the way it cuts up men."

"Don't make so much noise," Hua Hua said. "The rest of us haven't seen it yet."

On screen the two men finished their work, took the money, then received two more women, this time rather more imaginatively.

"You have to let men earn money," Hua Hua said to Lin Ying. "This film's not too bad, lets off steam."

Lin Ying could feel her face getting hot. "Those are pretty strong men."

Shao Liuliu folded her arms over her chest. "Don't

go adoring Westerners. The assets of some Chinese men are a lot more substantial than theirs."

Lin Ying knew Shao Liuliu was waiting for her to ask how she knew, and she wanted to ask but couldn't. Instead she turned to Hua Hua. "Where'd you get this video?"

Shao Liuliu giggled. "No need to say, Hua Hua. It's bound to have come from Qi Jun—he's a real collector. Relies on the vast good fortune of his illustrious and influential father."

"You're right. Who but he has the means to get this kind of thing?" Customs severely prohibited pornography, and anyone smuggling it was fined and imprisoned. Confiscated tapes found their way into the hands of high-level cadres and their sons, so that watching pornographic videos had become a special cultural privilege of the elite.

Lin Ying said, "Qi Jun lives a carefree life."

"I've heard that in late May someone was pressing him to pay a debt he owed of a hundred thousand *yuan*. Fortunately the 'disturbance' started and it was easy for him to hide." Shao Liuliu poked Hua Hua as she said this. "Don't cover up for your new lover. Isn't that right?"

Hua Hua didn't deny the word *lover*. She gestured lightly in the air and said, "I don't think he has the guts to play around with that kind of money."

Now the video was showing the two men servicing a woman in a remarkable way. The three women stared silently at this creative scene. When it finished, they all but drew a deep breath in unison on behalf of the men.

"I like seeing men waiting on women, being their slaves." Shao Liuliu turned from the screen to Lin Ying with a smile. "Little Lin, I'll tell you something that will make you laugh. The Degraded Survivors' Club had a bet: who could lay Lin Ying first."

Stunned, Lin Ying turned around to her quickly. What would the next insult be?

1 0

"Who?" she asked.

"Some men." Shao Liuliu was unconcerned.

"Which men?" Lin Ying picked up her glass and took a gulp. "Was Li Jiangjiang in on it?"

Shao Liuliu hadn't expected her to be so direct or so serious. She stopped for a moment, then said, "No, not him."

"How do you know?"

Shao Liuliu said Yan Yan had told her. She switched the subject and started talking about the suicide of Yan Yan's wife, Douzi, in the winter. Douzi had worshiped the man she considered a poetic genius. She'd been devoted to him, had sacrificed herself for him, and this turned Yan Yan against her. Once when they were arguing, he said angrily, "If you want to die, go ahead and die." That night she cut the arteries in her groin and bled to death in bed.

"Yan Yan was so heartbroken he came running over to tell me. I comforted him for a while but then told him that with Douzi's body not even cold yet I just didn't have the heart to go further. So he left. Not a week later I saw him in the East Wind market with a young girl with a ponytail on his arm." Shao Liuliu snorted. "Degraded pedants!" She lit a cigarette. "Nan An, that round-faced novelist in our school, told me which women novelists and poets in China are considered degenerate."

Hua Hua showed some interest. "Tell us, Liuliu, who was on it?"

"He said, Mei Yan of the northwest, Xiao Hong of Beijing, Li Wenping of Shanghai, Zhang Qing, a whole list. What does 'degenerate' mean? I asked him. He said, 'Willing to sell their bodies in order to get published and be famous.' "

"That's funny—you mean the editors and critics aren't even more degenerate? Who's worse, the prostitute or the one who goes whoring? Why is it women who always take the rap?" asked Hua Hua.

"Isn't that the truth. They say a few bad things about me, too." Shao Liuliu seemed to be pouring out her grievances tonight. "They say I have reasons for going with this one, then with that one. Of course I have reasons, but it's not the kind they talk about."

Lin Ying did not like the discussion. Her name was probably on Nan An's list, and she wasn't sure she wanted to know the details. But Shao Liuliu's discussion of the bet stayed with her like a deep inner bruise, a hurt that wouldn't go away. Li Jiangjiang might very well have joined in the bet. If so, the tiny bit of "purity" she clung to in her own mind was a joke.

He couldn't have, she thought to herself, but then again, why not? Who knew what was going on with people in this world? Li Jiangjiang was someone she couldn't see into, especially in this chaotic time. Reality was not like a poem in which she could select exactly the word she wanted to use.

Beer in hand, she had long ago stopped watching the next video. She had no desire to watch further—

the women playing with men on the screen were the opposite of real life.

Hua Hua looked at Lin Ying, raised her glass, and lightly twirled about as she announced, with a smile on her face, "Here's to the men who loyally wait on women! You know, of course, that prostitutes come in four kinds: men servicing men, men servicing women, women servicing women, and women servicing men. Our culture, damn it all, only recognizes the last. In fact, there are far fewer good gigolos than good essayists." Hua Hua emphasized this with dramatic gestures. She had found a good subject to emote about. She continued. "The more experienced we are, the more we realize that men are, in fact, afraid of women. Some are secretly afraid, some quite open about it. Think of it: what can be more awful than a truly self-confident woman facing a deflated man who has lost it, a shriveled, lifeless little worm?"

"Marvelous!" Shao Liuliu applauded.

Lin Ying thought of her own first time. What had been a painful and undisclosable secret episode in her past had just been turned on its head. She drew a long breath and felt a great deal better.

"Let's not allow men the privilege of using us for their amusement," said Shao Liuliu. "Let's make a few bets on them! Who's willing to give Wu Wei an initiation?"

"Give that meddling old lady of his something to really get hot about!"

"Who wants to deflower Yan Heituo?"

"Big Beard is pretty good at playing around, but I'm afraid, as they say in the opera, he's a spear with a wax point."

"What about Nan An? Yan Yan?"

Shao Liuliu looked down her nose at these suggestions. Both men, she said, were spineless braggarts.

Outside, the leaves rustled. A breeze lifted the curtains from time to time, blowing them in as if to accompany the merriment.

Lin Ying had never talked like this before. She certainly had never made fun of these illustrious men, these new stars in China's literary firmament, men destined to leave their mark on history, after all. It was pretty daring to scoff at these radiant beings. Only Beijing's leading female talents could talk so disdainfully. It made her supremely happy.

But she herself stayed mostly silent. Her life had been a long conversation with herself—whether about resentments or hopes, the dialogue went on within her and stayed there. But these two Beijing women! Hua Hua's incisive verdicts were exactly what she needed to counter the poison inside her. She hadn't seen Shao Liuliu much before, had only heard people say she was too liberated, insolent in a rather unfeminine way. But today Lin Ying found her candor a gift. She ached to share the clear sense of superiority these two women enjoyed.

11

Someone knocked.

"Come in!" Hua Hua cried. Li Jiangjiang pushed open the door and stepped in.

"We were just getting to you," Hua Hua said, "and see, the brave volunteer arrives!"

He didn't even look at Hua Hua but charged straight for Lin Ying. "What are you doing out like this so late! You didn't say a word to me! These aren't normal times. There are soldiers everywhere . . ."

Lin Ying heard nothing but the tone of his voice, like that of an adult scolding a child. The spark smoldering inside her burst into flame. "Who told you to look after me anyway? Know what I mean? You've already been relieved of that responsibility!"

Li Jiangjiang turned pale. He was not eager to discuss in front of Hua Hua and Shao Liuliu what had happened just two hours earlier. He stalled for a moment, then changed his tone, and—conciliatory now—said, "I was just worried about your safety."

Shao Liuliu stood up. "Jiangjiang, you've come at just the right time. Here we are, we three women, with no one to keep us company. Come help us test whether or not our theory is correct. First let's watch a video to see a demonstration of the movements."

Only then did Li Jiangjiang notice what was on the screen: a man with his back to the camera was in the process of obeying his female client's instructions, with his tongue.

"You're watching this kind of thing?" His face turned red.

"Why not? Is it only for men?"

"In the West, only the lowest of the low watch this kind of trash," he said.

Shao Liuliu and Hua Hua attacked together. "What do we know about 'the West'? You're the only expert on that. Right now, in China, only the highest ranks of male officials get to watch this."

"And we women, if we so much as glance at it, are liable to end up in prison or have our heads chopped off!"

Li Jiangjiang knew that he had stirred up a hornet's nest, that he was not up to sparring with these two.

"You should do your best to study more, to keep us ladies from getting upset."

Lin Ying was sitting, glass in hand, a faint smile on her face. Li Jiangjiang went over to her and pulled her up, dragging her by the arm out the door and into the corridor.

Lin Ying pulled loose. "Let go, you're hurting me."

"I never thought you'd all be making fun of me." Li Jiangjiang's voice shook with anger. "Lin, pull yourself together. Don't self-destruct. Don't throw yourself away!"

"So you've learned the same tune as Chen Yu! He scolds me for being shameless. You tell me not to self-destruct." Lin Ying was vehement. "I've made yet another mistake."

"Mistake? What have I done?" Li Jiangjiang was furious.

"Your mistake was to let me get to know you!"

His face hardened. The hallway was dim but his expression was absolutely clear. After several long seconds, the corner of his mouth twitched, but still he said nothing. No matter how you read it, her words were grim.

Lin Ying stood there watching him. Time passed painfully. Then she could no longer stand it. She hadn't wanted to say this but couldn't stop herself, and she tried to make it sound light and gentle. "Jiangjiang, tonight I'll stay here with Hua Hua. You don't have to wait for me, okay?"

Li Jiangjiang pulled her around by the shoulder. He was doing his utmost to control himself. "Is this your final decision? Is it in earnest?"

Lin Ying took a step back. "All my decisions are in earnest," she said.

He looked at her, incredulous, then nodded. His hand fell as he turned and bolted down the stairs.

Lin Ying stood in the hallway for a moment. When she turned around she saw the two women standing in the doorway, astonished. They had not imagined their little game would have such immediate results.

The video was over. Lin Ying went back in the room and picked up her glass. Hua Hua came to fill it, then helped herself and Shao Liuliu to more. Lin Ying lifted her glass to the two of them, then fiercely threw back her head and drained it.

3

14 JULY 1989

FRIDAY

1

Wu Wei took off his glasses and used his finger to wipe the dust from the lenses. Then he put them on again and pushed them back up his nose. He tried once more to comprehend Lin Ying's poem.

One more time: abundant perceptions of a
Full stop. Watching the sound of trumpets vibrating
    against red flags. And I ask,
Why are they only able to succeed in the dead of night?
Why do you want to stick this elegy in my hair
    it is a silver needle. Yes, it is a bullet
    but only through this can the core be removed, forever:
    sucking out our heaviness, forever:
    sucking out impressions of us till we are pure. Yet
The pupils in your eyes are speaking

Wu Wei said he had never read this kind of poem before. He felt it was . . . not without meaning.

Everything returns to silence, no longer is there poetry,
only the frantic sweeping up: I write of a different time
   and—

"It ends just like that?" Wu Wei was surprised.

"Just like that. With a dash. An inconclusive conclusion."

"I admit I don't really get it." He pushed his glasses back again, trying not to look embarrassed. He himself had become famous in the early 1980s, when he was criticized for writing poetry that was incomprehensible.

"If you understand me," said Lin Ying, "you can understand my poetry. And as soon as the poem is understood it becomes prose; if you understand me, then I become prose to you."

Wu Wei stared at her. "Leave a woman for three days and when you see her again you have to gaze in admiration. Where have you been getting such an abstruse line?"

Lin Ying leaned back against the bench. "Can't a poet learn it for herself?" Her hair was pulled back with a ribbon; a few loose strands hung down around her ears. "Poetry is simply the rebellious essence of language itself."

Lin Ying seemed almost in a trance. Wu Wei watched her so intently that he didn't notice when one of the papers he was holding slipped to the ground. "Splendid. The person, the poetry, more and more mysterious. So what you say is that it's probably better not to understand you."

"You've got it." Lin Ying bent over to pick up the paper. She was wearing a black skirt that came to her knees and a pair of sandals. Crows flew from branch to branch of the trees, their black shadows flashing among the green leaves.

Wu Wei and Lin Ying sat at the highest point of the park. The day slowly turned from pale blue to pale yellow. The sun was intense but hidden in the haze. Cicadas announced themselves wildly from all directions, forcing people to recognize their existence and also to acknowledge how hot it was. It was the hottest part of summer in Beijing. The clamor of the city, carried along on waves of heat, pressed constantly on everyone, jangling their nerves. New and old buildings of every kind, built up against the ancient palace walls and watchtowers, looked like wooden blocks piled helter-skelter by a child—colorless, painted in a range of muddy hues. One could just make out the straight lines of broad avenues cutting through the jumble of architectural forms. Traffic moved along these lines as the mighty army of demonstrators had done only three months earlier. She had chanted stirring slogans with the demonstrators back then, had sung the blood-tingling "Internationale," had used the power of the crowd to escape her own problems. When she wasn't marching, she was immersing herself in the activities at the square, talking all day to people—without even using her own words.

Now, she used her own language to speak, but it was hard to find a response. What her poems were about was already in the poems; it was unnecessary and impossible to explain further. Wu Wei considered himself a poet of some achievement, so he should be able to read poetry and understand it. Of course, he might have grasped a trace of the meaning and seen the direction but not been brave enough to follow it to the end.

The pressures on her increased.

2

Hua Hua said she was now in love with the the *Book of Changes* and could tell fortunes with coins. She couldn't predict the future, but she did at least know whether events in the next few days would be auspicious or not. For example, in late May her hexagrams had repeatedly predicted calamities—unfortunately nobody would listen and even she didn't pay much attention.

"All right, is it auspicious or not to go out today?" Lin Ying stuffed some of her poetry into her satchel.

"Of course. How else could I make a date with you? Be there at eight o'clock sharp. Don't be late!" Hua Hua was wearing a black bra and sitting before a mirror combing her hair.

At the sight of her near-naked body, Lin Ying said candidly, "Your back is truly beautiful!"

"Lin Ying, my little alluring spirit." Hua Hua laughed at her. "Tell me, why don't you want to have your fortune told? You can't not care about it at all!"

"I try hard not to tell the future," Lin Ying responded, "to avoid having too many disappointments, too many unfulfilled hopes. But if it makes Miss Hua happy, I'm willing to try cards."

Hua Hua pulled a pack of cards from a drawer. Lin Ying extracted the four kings, lined them up in a row on the table, and carefully shuffled the rest of the deck three times. She said, very seriously, "You can think about this without saying anything out loud. Consider these cards as four men that you know, but don't tell me who they are. Remember them. I'll think of four men myself and see how they come out."

Lin Ying let Hua Hua pull out four cards at random and put them over the four kings. She kept the rest of the cards in her left hand. Hua Hua watched as Lin Ying turned over the cards one by one.

The first king got the jack of spades. "A small man," Lin Ying said, "up to all kinds of tricks." Hua Hua nodded: That makes sense.

The second king got the nine of diamonds. "He's cocky, has an exaggerated opinion of himself, doesn't know his limits."

The third king was capped with the queen of clubs. "There's a woman hanging on him all the time, a tyrant—poor bastard has a hard time."

The fourth king had an ace of diamonds.

"What's this?"

"Making his escape."

"Right! Right!" Hua Hua said happily. "I'll watch out! What about you, now?"

"How can the one getting her fortune told say it isn't right?" Lin Ying felt a vague sense of unease. "Forget it. That's enough. You shouldn't dig too deeply into heavenly secrets." She put down the cards.

"All right, we'll leave it at that. But could you put names to them?" Hua Hua asked.

"Once you do that, there's no way to influence things—the die is cast."

"Well, anyway. I'll name the ones I can identify. The last is Li Jiangjiang, right? Is he really going to go?"

Lin Ying nodded. She picked up a tape lying by the tape recorder, the piece Shao Liuliu was most proud of, "Thousand Mountains, Cold Moon," which Shao Liuliu had left for them. She put it in the machine. The sounds of a lute filled the room. Moonlight flowed down the flanks of a mountain; like water released into a pool, skeins of wild geese flew by.

SEVERAL DAYS earlier, Li Jiangjiang had come to visit Lin Ying with a telegram in hand. He asked if she would come see him off at the train station: his parents had asked him to come back home to Jilin for a brief while—they wanted to see him before he left China. Listening to his earnest entreaty, Lin Ying smiled, and he had smiled, too. They hadn't spoken for over half a month.

They took a bus together to the train station. It was after rush hour, and there were only a few passengers in the front seats. Lin Ying chose the last row and sat by the window. Li Jiangjiang sat to her right, putting his one small bag on an empty seat. He told her about his new ambition: to put aside literary theory and switch to management. In China, literary people were too isolated. Political types found it all too easy to use them as a target, to say they were troublemakers who had to be whipped into obedience, while the public thought that their problems were all due to their being overexcitable and emotional. Anyone involved in literature in China was bound to come to an unhappy end.

"China's future lies in slowly creating a middle class. When there are more people with money, there will be democracy," Li Jiangjiang said conclusively.

Lin Ying let him spout one argument after another, then reminded him, "You were once so infatuated with literary theory—is it so easy to give it up?"

In order to have a secure livelihood abroad, a base to live on, he was willing to change his occupation to something with more of a future, he said.

"What you mean is that to be a writer in China is too hard, and outside China a writer is too poor?"

"You get the whole point with just one little hint! Well, you can go abroad too!"

Li Jiangjiang had been waiting for her to ask to go with him, and since she hadn't, he was suggesting it himself. Lin Ying did not take the bait. "I'm a poet, a Chinese-language poet. Even if our culture thinks of a poet as some kind of strange beast, it would be hard for me to change my stripes, I think. And I don't want to, anyway."

Li Jiangjiang looked embarrassed, said he didn't mean anything like that, didn't want to force anyone, but if Lin Ying wanted to go abroad he'd be only too happy to help her.

He had been holding Lin Ying's hand, and now she pulled it back. The bus route was the same they had taken by bicycle when Li Jiangjiang had first taken her to his dorm, but today they were going in the opposite direction.

"If you want to survive, you have to forget some things," Li Jiangjiang said. "Before, you were the one trying to comfort me and calm me down."

"I'm afraid you *can* be calm, but I can't." Lin Ying threw him a look. "Since the disturbance, my periods haven't been normal." Instinctively she clapped a hand over her mouth. "How could I have used the word *disturbance*?"

How is it we never learn? We hear others say it— disturbance, disturbance—day after day, so we get used to it. The pestilence of amnesia starts in the capital, then spreads like a contagion throughout the country. People so desperately want a new beginning, to be safe and secure, to go back to business. In the end, am I different from anyone else? She was in despair.

Beijing was fully immersed in the summer heat. Martial-law troops stood guard at every major inter-section, patrolling the overpasses with special care. Armed with loaded rifles, soldiers stood every two or three meters, at each railing post, motionless as stone statues under their helmets. Each of them was streaming with sweat, which ran down from their scalps, past their ears, over their foreheads, down their necks.

Li Jiangjiang turned from the window to Lin Ying. "You could write your poetry abroad. At least if you wanted to you could: freedom is a precious thing."

Lin Ying shook her head. "Here there are people listening, but one can't speak. There one can speak, but nobody listens."

"You're still looking at things from the traditional

Chinese viewpoint, aren't you? You think that mere words and culture can modernize China. China has to start at the instrumental level, not with metaphysics."

"Earlier you spoke for yourself, now you speak for China! Earlier you talked about spiritual freedom, and now you talk about material conditions! The fact is, you don't have to explain yourself. I'm just being completely selfish. I'd rather have people hate me. I'm just not willing to be a poet no one pays attention to."

He didn't want her to go on. "All right, all right."

Lin Ying kept her hands on her knees. The bus was going along Jianguomen Avenue. She looked out; people were beginning to leave work, bicycles were flowing by like water, and there were trolley buses, cars, and taxis everywhere. One after another, imposing buildings marched by, more and more of them. When the bus turned the corner, she turned to look again at Li Jiangjiang.

He took her hand back and caressed it lightly. He was a very open-minded man, he said, and after he had gone, Lin Ying could do what she wanted with his friends. There was one exception.

"Who?"

"Chen Yu."

"Why?"

"Because he's my . . ." Li Jiangjiang stopped for a moment. "Because he's now on the opposite side from me and my friends."

Lin Ying looked out the window again. Li Jiangjiang had his pride; he couldn't stand to be insulted. "What you've just said is simply too funny!"

"Think as you wish. Anyone else is fine, but not Chen Yu!" Li Jiangjiang's intensity was palpable.

Did she really need to argue for some kind of authorization to be with Chen Yu? Lin Ying decided to remain silent. She felt as dark as the shadows thrown by the downtown buildings: what right did men have to make this kind of demand of women?

LIN YING didn't tell Hua Hua any of this after their fortune-telling session. She picked up her satchel and said that she'd be going, she had a meeting. "What direction is auspicious today?" she said, to tease Hua Hua.

Hua Hua picked up some coins and read their position, then looked up in a book: "South. South is 'greatly auspicious.'"

Lin Ying said that she was going toward the southwest. Hua Hua said that was fine, just so she went in a southerly direction.

3

And so she went to Altar Park to see Wu Wei.

Since the start of the month, many newspapers and magazines had been suspended or shut down altogether. The news industry had been declared a disaster zone that had to undergo major "rectification." Wu Wei and Chen Yu were in the same key unit undergoing the most intense reorganization. Lin Ying had heard that Wu Wei had run into problems, that he'd actually been fired because of his activities during the disturbance, that he was now being asked to write a "self-criticism." No doubt he needed to get out and talk to someone, divert himself from depression. She hoped she could help him.

But as soon as they met, Wu Wei told her Chen Yu had been put in prison and was under investigation. He and Chen Yu worked together; Chen Yu was his boss.

The sudden news was a shock. Chen Yu always did things steadily, unlike Wu Wei, who was liable to get involved in complications. If the authorities caught anyone, Chen Yu was the last person it would be.

"He wrote articles supporting the students. So what? There were millions of articles like that. He demonstrated in the streets? There were plenty of reporters demonstrating. What's more, he even tried to persuade the students to go back to their schools."

Wu Wei laughed, "That was exactly his mistake. He gave the students bad advice—retreating to the universities was the worst idea he could possibly have come up with. If the students had done that, it would have meant they'd won."

"Why?"

"You still don't know? If the students went back to school, the government would lose its excuse for quashing them. Then how could they hope to deal with all the political groups that had mushroomed overnight? How could they teach a lesson to the 'rioters'? It's hard, though," Wu Wei continued, "to put a name on this crime of giving students a pernicious idea. So they grabbed another handle to get him: indecent behavior, hooliganism."

"Chen Yu a hooligan? I don't believe it. I know him too well." To her, this sounded like another internal battle in those huge organizations, one faction looking endlessly for some pretext to get at another.

"I'm afraid it's precisely because you know him so well that he's in trouble."

"What do you mean? What connection does this have to me?"

She knew that Chen Yu had kept her letters, and also the photographs they had taken at the square, but if it came to danger, Chen Yu would have burned them—he was very quick. He wouldn't sit there stupidly waiting for them to come destroy him.

"What kind of indecent behavior?"

"Sleeping with two women at the same time."

She stood up, shocked. "What slander!"

"I don't believe it, either. Where would you ever find two women willing to do it face to face?" Wu Wei hesitated, as though he found it hard to say all this straight out but had to. "It's said that one of the two women was his wife, the other was you, that somebody informed on him. I don't know who."

She might have been stunned by this, but instead Lin Ying was less angry than she had been before. Indeed she was calm. Since she knew it wasn't true, at least she could understand the situation a little more clearly.

Wu Wei now became agitated. "You'd think that China's intellectuals would be a little more resolute this time. Not come down to this kind of Cultural Revolution trick, incriminating everyone in sight in order to save themselves. But look what happens: the moment one is caught, he informs on someone else, and on it goes. Mao Zedong said Chinese intellectuals were weaklings by nature. Seems this is as true now as it ever was."

Lin Ying suddenly remembered the evening a month earlier when Chen Yu had said things that decisively broke off their relationship. She remembered most clearly the phrase "Our relationship ends here. Don't come looking for me after this."

He may have put me off intentionally, she thought, to keep me from being pulled into this whirlpool. Perhaps what had happened had kept him from explaining the danger, and all he could do was fake a cold exterior. This possibility hurt, the moment she thought of it.

THE LAST day she and Chen Yu had been at Tiananmen Square together, he'd been determined to get to the students' command headquarters, which had been set up at the Memorial monument. "I've got to get there, tell the leaders it's time to retreat. They have to do it now. If they hold off any longer there's going to be big trouble—politics requires knowing when to pull back." She agreed with him and the two of them had pressed forward, but the students' defense line blocked their way. Without authorized passes, they couldn't approach the headquarters.

They had retreated to the northwest corner of the square. Chen Yu had been extremely upset and had told her, "Intellectuals have been working for ten years to enlighten the nation in a rational way. Another few years and there will be real results. But if it comes to a fight, everything will be gone in a day." He decided to put on his *People's Daily* badge and try his luck. "Wait here. Don't move!" Within a few seconds he had disappeared in the crowd.

Slogans were being chanted in all directions; performances, broadcasts, all kinds of news and information were blowing in the wind. Banners protruded from the tops of wave upon wave of tents; a siren wailed shrilly, as an ambulance tried to part the crowd in order to carry out a student who had fainted from hunger. There was the sound of running feet, of shouts of rescue. There were people publicly renouncing their membership in the Communist Party. The largest open square in the world had become the world's most intimate breeding ground for rumors and misinformation. More than a million people were passing out information all day long, and nobody could prove or disprove a single item of it, one way or another. Lin Ying's mouth was dry, her tongue parched. From time to time she listened to the debates: most of the students were in favor of sticking it out, saying retreat was a display of weakness. But plenty of people were fearful: if they pulled back to the schools, they could be picked off and arrested, one by one, as counterrevolutionaries.

Chen Yu returned after an hour or more, downcast, his forehead bruised. Lin Ying pushed past the people who were arguing with him. Gently she stroked his forehead, asking anxiously, "What happened?"

"Don't worry, it's nothing." Chen Yu shook away her hand. The student leaders had refused to talk anymore; he had been pulled down off the memorial. They wanted him to "obey democracy, submit to democracy." What kind of democracy was that! The vote of a few representatives from various faculties! "I told them," Chen Yu said, "without a real debate there's no real democracy. In conditions like this, the more a school representative takes an activist, hard-line approach, the more exposure and publicity he gets. They don't know that compromise is what really takes courage. They got angry, said I was betraying their exalted ideals."

The two of them hung their heads in silence. After that, Chen Yu never went to the square again. He said that the Chinese always claimed to follow the principle of the golden mean, but no one in politics was willing to. The student leaders were saying they wanted to force the government to lay its cards on the table, that things would never get so bad as to lead to bloodshed. They didn't realize that the authorities' best hope was for a single decisive operation to finish the affair. They didn't want to muddy the water, have things dangling that they'd later regret; already they had silenced the people in the Party who had a different opinion. Playing politics had become a huge gamble.

Lin Ying had listened quietly. Compared with Chen Yu, she was an outsider when it came to politics, which basically she knew nothing about. Strictly in terms of politics, Chen Yu was undoubtedly right—but did she personally really want to pull out? Not necessarily. The moment that happened, she would feel empty, lost. Only on Tiananmen Square, in the midst of that tragedy affecting everyone, could she forget her own individual tragedy. This was something worth holding on to—a reason for living, in fact.

"Better not go," Chen Yu told her. "You're a poet. Haven't you always said politics is no good for poetry? Well, let me tell you, poets are no good in politics, either."

This injunction upset her, and the two of them had parted, thinking different thoughts.

At the square, she heard poems by her classmate Yi

Dafu recited over the loudspeaker so passionately that it made her uncomfortable. You might as well shout slogans as recite that kind of poetry. On the other hand, the rock stars made everyone happy, and she watched Yan Heituo and the others perform for the first time. They sang with their electric guitars, the square echoed with their sounds over the loudspeakers, and tens of thousands of people joined in singing with them. This was unforgettable, better than anything she had ever seen. Unfortunately, they performed at the square only that once.

For a while, Lin Ying actually did avoid the square, staying home at the dormitory, reading for two whole days. She heard that the Beijing students at the square were mostly pulling out, that those still camped there were mainly new arrivals from other cities. Perhaps Chen Yu's advice and that of other intellectuals was being accepted. Chen Yu seemed to have become involved in high-level emergency discussions and it was not easy for him to tell her what was happening. It had already been several days since she had been to his place. Mainly, she wanted to calm herself down, wipe her mind clean of all concerns.

Then, on the evening of 3 June, Beijing was put on alert through loudspeakers and radio broadcasts. Citizens were warned that they were to stay off the streets, that anyone on the streets that evening would be considered a counterrevolutionary. Her heart started to pound; she simply had to go to the square. She could not talk about some kind of golden mean when armored tanks were advancing on Tiananmen. Her friends, her colleagues were there. She could not stand by, hands in sleeves. She telephoned Chen Yu. He told her not to go. He said this was a power struggle that was already over, and the students at the square did not understand democracy. You don't need to "understand" democracy, she thought, in order to fight for it. Democracy might be a concept but, even more, it was a kind of dream flowing through your veins.

Many thought as she did. They poured out—old men, old women, children, on bicycles, carts, motorcycles, in taxis, buses, people wearing shorts, T-shirts, wearing sandals, walking the streets. In the tide of people Lin Ying never hesitated. She headed for the square in that beautiful-as-ever summer's evening.

`NOBODY TRUSTS anyone. Just look out for yourself. I wonder if it was Chen Yu's wife who exposed him. Of course, there's no assurance Chen Yu won't hand you over, either," Wu Wei was saying.

Every syllable pierced Lin Ying to the core. "Hand me over for indecent behavior?" she retorted, furious. "That I can deal with easily, and I can speak for Chen Yu, too."

"That's the hard part—you can explain away the indecent behavior, but then he can still be accused on political grounds. If you try to clarify one, they'll focus on the other. It's a two-edged sword—it'll get you either way."

Lin Ying had never imagined that problems would become so grave. She put both feet solidly on the ground and pressed her hands to the bench on either side. If that's the way it was, perhaps the students had been right. They were definitely right if the authorities were trying to eliminate even such moderate people as Chen Yu.

Wu Wei reached out with his right hand and brushed away a leaf that had fallen on Lin Ying's hair. His tone became very familiar. "You're innocent, I know that. I believe it."

"What? How?" Lin Ying shot back. It occurred to her that Wu Wei might well have been the person who exposed Chen Yu and, precisely because of that, to show his innocence had been the first to race over and tell her the news.

"I believe it," Wu Wei repeated firmly. He paused for a moment, looked right and left. "I hadn't realized this park could be so quiet."

4

A stack of poems was on the bench between them. Wu Wei now groped to his left to pick it up, and his body seemed to have found an excuse to move a little closer to Lin Ying.

The martial-law troops of Beijing had given no indication of leaving. Twenty years seemed to have passed in the weeks since 4 June, but it also seemed like a day. Many things were now vaguely reminiscent of the old days, the only difference being that so many people had learned to sweep the snow only in front of their own doors. A new wave of cultural officials took up their posts and got industriously to work: propaganda tools, television, newspapers, magazines were set in motion extolling the morality of Communism; all of China again became a nation of "ethical gentlemen."

"You believe that what about me is clean? My politics or my lifestyle?"

"I don't know about politics myself." Wu Wei smiled deprecatingly. "I believe, certainly, that you are a girl of pure heart." Again he moved closer.

Lin Ying frowned. It wasn't discovering his intentions that bothered her. It was his style of courtship, flattering her with the word *pure*, adding *certainly* to the argument. This style of seduction was discomfiting.

"How do you know?" she demanded.

"I know it from your poetry."

"Didn't you just say you couldn't understand my poetry! Now I'm an extremely liberated woman, very, very liberated," she said provocatively, rudely. Wu Wei was known as a proper sort of person, a perfectly faithful husband. Could he have heard this rumor of three in a bed and thought she was sexually promiscuous, an easy lay, and have come here to try her out? She had never been so angry with all the hypocrisy, false decency, fake respectability.

"I am, in fact, quite a loose woman!" she declared. She got up and stood, her legs apart in an aggressive pose, right in front of him. "You like loose women, don't you?"

Involuntarily Wu Wei rose, his eyes avoiding hers. He blushed, and after a long while stammered, "Me? Of course not."

"Take a good look at yourself. Men love purity, but purity's not enough—not enough flavor, nothing to sink your teeth into. What men want is purity overlaying a little licentiousness, which they can pull out like a drawer when they want it, shut it when they don't."

Wu Wei laughed awkwardly. "How did we get to

this point?" He had never imagined Lin Ying would be so aggressive, he told her, and he was tired of dealing with people's complexities. He shook his head. "Everyone said the mountain girl has strength, and today I've seen it in action. But we're just friends, Lin Ying, okay?"

"Sure, sure." Lin Ying bent down to get her poetry. She put it in her satchel, said she had to be going, had to see Hua Hua.

Fragrant Altar Park was silent and cool under the leafy trees, and no one was in sight. When Lin Ying and Wu Wei had gotten there, they'd seen only three men with Western jackets; from the sound of their accents they were from outside Beijing, here on business. Local people didn't dare come out to a park yet. The two of them made their way down the stone staircase to the pavilion, supporting themselves against the grotesque rock formations lining the way placed there artificially like mute witnesses to history. Dusk was falling, a few pastel evening clouds dotted the sky, ripples in the pond below reflected the same hues.

At the bottom of the twisting stone stairs, the two of them walked toward the gate to the park. Wu Wei took Lin Ying's hand. "I truly like you . . . your poems," he said. "If I still had any power I'd make sure they were published in prominent journals and publicize your new, mysteriously restrained style. Poems— But right now the only thing we can do is let this poetry hide away, like a recluse in the mountains. It's really a shame."

Lin Ying did not pull her hand away. "Thank you," she said. "But my poetry is not about a new style or any new school." They reached the entrance. "About

Chen Yu. What do you think I ought to do?" She wanted to gauge his attitude.

"Best not to do anything. It doesn't officially involve you so don't go throwing yourself into the net. You can't save him. Nobody can save him. Don't forget China's 'special national situation.' "

His pace slowed and he resumed his usual man-of-letters air. Looking at a black sedan parked by the road, he sighed. "From one kind of darkness to another." The low houses by the side of the park looked like caskets, he said. "Remember, we mustn't be blind or impetuous. The more careful the better. Don't let anyone get a handle on you. Keep a low profile, live a secluded life, don't go out too much. Be careful in everything you do."

He didn't say a word about the self-criticism he'd been forced to write. He really is a good-hearted person, Lin Ying thought to herself. "Don't worry," she answered. "I'll keep my tail tucked between my legs."

5

Lin Ying took the bus to Forest Slope.

The news that Chen Yu had been arrested cut like a blade through the love-hate history that had been weighing on her. Any feelings of love had shattered in that moment when she saw him with Mei Ling, and after that it was impossible to go back to the way things had been. But still, there were other emotions between them, cultivated over a long period of time. She felt that her relations with Chen Yu were now much simpler: whether or not he had incriminated her, she was still his friend.

Her mistake had been in taking physical love as the

foundation of the relationship between a man and a woman, she decided. That put the man in a contrary position to the woman, which required him to play all kinds of devious tricks. Lin Ying felt she was much clearer about all this now: friendship was mutually established, whereas sex was, quite rightly, a matter pertaining solely to the individual self.

The east-west bus route passed along the Avenue of Eternal Peace. It was forbidden now to stop at Tiananmen, but two cars in front were driving extremely slowly and the bus also slowed down. "Look at the Memorial monument! Look at the Memorial monument!" a husky peasant beside her was saying to his son. People in the bus were looking this way and that —toward the Revolutionary History Museum to the east, the Mao Zedong Memorial Hall behind the Memorial monument, the Great Hall of the People to the west. They all seemed heavy and cumbersome, with the vast cleanliness of the square between them. The emptiness was spine-tingling. Not a person around except soldiers with rifles.

To the north, in front of the Gate of Heavenly Peace, a group of off-duty soldiers took turns striking poses as they snapped each other's photographs. Flashbulbs were popping. The huge portrait of Mao Zedong still hanging above the gate looked brand-new. Most of the soldiers on duty in Beijing had been summoned from the countryside; they wanted to show radiant and happy countenances in the photographs they sent home. But the faces of the soldiers still on duty were as severe and immobile as if glazed with ice. Lin Ying was standing near the bus conductor, hanging on to a strap. She turned her head away from the scene and let her eyes rest on the skylight above her, encrusted with grime.

In the failing light the massive Avenue of Eternal Peace seemed cold and empty. Everyone was waiting for history to clean things up, but history was taking its time; it was far better than humans at waiting. She must now be decisive, take responsibility for her own actions; perhaps it truly had to be that way. Before, she had not been able to resist the seductive power of the square. She had wanted to escape her pain and failure, wanted to run from the desolation love had brought her; she had lacked the courage to face herself.

Now the problems are easier and simpler, she thought: mere indecent behavior. Women seemed terrified of the accusation of being loose but willing to make the accusation of other women; women were used by men and women alike as an excuse for all kinds of sins, to the point that when a man was arrested and locked up, so-called law enforcers could automatically make a woman the cause of his downfall.

People got off at the next stop and a seat became empty. She sat down and put her satchel on her knees. More people got on; the bus became crowded and the heavy stench of sweat hung in the air. She had to point her nose at the window to catch the slight breeze.

ɪ ᴛ ᴡ ᴀ s eight-thirty by the time Lin Ying got to Forest Slope. When Hua Hua had invited her to this place, she had only said, mysteriously, that tonight she would be doing "creative modeling." She told her to be on time in order to help her move the creative spirit.

Qi Jun answered the door. He was outfitted and coiffed like an artist, a trim beard framing his lower face but without a moustache, hair manelike and falling to his shoulders. Above his thick black-rimmed glasses the hair made him look less like a lion than like a caricature of a lion. Lin Ying always thought this whenever she saw Qi Jun.

"You're late," he said as he let her in. "But also just in time. Hua Hua and I are at an impasse. You've got to help us think of something." He held out his hands to show her the paint drips on his work clothes. How could a painter get himself so smeared? she wondered. Across the hall, two spotlit easels were propped against the wall. There was a faint coolness in the building, perhaps because of the luxuriant trees and lawn just outside, that you felt as soon as you walked in.

She had been in this suite of rooms before. It was difficult to call it Qi Jun's home—he had a number of apartments, each with its own purpose, and friends often borrowed them. This one was spacious, with a broad passageway connecting four rooms, of which two faced east, each with its own balcony. There was a toilet and shower, a kitchen with gas, heating, hot water, everything. The inside room, the largest, Qi Jun used as his painting studio. The pale gray floor tiles were polished to a reflective sheen. The room was rather austere, only two black chairs, a floor-length window that opened to the balcony, off-white curtains that had been gathered to the side. Along the wall was a comfortable-looking black leather sofa with a smoked-glass table in front of it. On the wall was a dial that allowed you to modulate the light in the room. The whole effect was very fresh and cool and elegant.

Hua Hua stood in the middle of the studio. She shrugged her shoulders at Lin Ying and pursed her mouth. She was dressed in tight black leotards from head to toe and was dripping in black paint. Even her face and her hair, pulled back in a bun, and her bare feet were covered with paint. At first glance she looked like the corpse Lin Ying had seen that night in June.

Hua Hua did not explain, just pointed to the terrazzo floor, on which was spread a huge sheet of beautiful high-quality paper. On it was a chaotic mess of paint.

Hua Hua put her hands on her hips and evaluated this "painting." Not so good, her expression said. It seemed that the phrase had already been said a few times before.

Qi Jun paced back and forth in front of it, cocking his head to look at the paint. "You need to use a little more creativity," he said.

"Hey," Hua Hua snorted, "are you the painter or am I?"

Qi Jun didn't even raise his head to look at her. "I love it when a woman gets upset, a little provocative. Gives it all a bit of a charge." He raised his hands in a determined gesture. "All right, we'll try again. This time we'll start from the upper-left corner."

He rolled up the paper on the floor, wadded it into a ball, and threw it across the room into a bamboo wastebasket on the balcony. He wiped the floor clean, then took another sheet of paper and spread it out. After spraying it with water, he picked up a paint can and daubed Hua Hua's body in a few places, touching it up, then surveyed her closely and told her to lie on the paper. He put down the can and brush and bent over to pat her, instructing her to squirm a little.

"Dance," he intoned, as if praying. "Dance, so that the god of the arts will enter your body."

Hua Hua rolled around a little, then climbed up unhappily. "If the god of the arts looks like me right now, you can imagine what the art is going to look like."

Under Hua Hua's gyrations, the impression left on the paper this time was of large indistinct blobs, the paint now slowly spreading in the dampened paper. You could just make out the trace of a human figure, but mostly the "painting" was oddly shaped blotches and irregular overlappings. Lin Ying didn't want to dash their spirits, but this wasn't art. Qi Jun and Hua Hua were silent. Perhaps they, too, weren't sure. Perhaps they had gone overboard, fallen from the vessel of art.

Hua Hua frowned slightly. "I'm afraid it isn't working."

"I believe you've just got the feeling for it," Qi Jun said, "and once you've got the feeling, you've got hold of that whore called Inspiration. She pretends to meet up with you suddenly, to fall madly in love, but in fact she's been lurking on the corner waiting for you." His voice trailed off and he sat down on the floor, dispirited.

6

"Where did you learn this way of painting?" Lin Ying put down her satchel and sat on the couch.

Qi Jun said proudly, "It's not an artist's secret, it's a revelation from above."

"Shameless braggart." Hua Hua punctured his discourse. "He dreamed it up in bed one night. He was looking at the sheets, all wrinkled, and said the passion of a woman's body could produce a kind of art, said that this would really shake up the Beijing avant-garde. He was just sorry he hadn't thought of it earlier or he could have put it in the Experimentalists' Exhibit earlier this year, gotten a lot of publicity, been in the limelight by producing a true sensation. As it happened, the prize went to that performance artist, the young woman who borrowed her father's gun and shot a piece of glass— she also killed the whole exhibition."

"Not at all the same. The crowd was just making a lot of noise for effect. What we have here is art." Qi Jun bent over and pointed to various parts of the painting. "Look, here's the mysterious rhythm and charm of traditional Chinese painting. And here's the postmodern Western concept of lack of center. Salvador Dali and others used women's bodies to paint paintings before, but they weren't successful. First of all, they didn't have our wonderful paper, but more important, they didn't have a Chinese woman! Painting is a kind of body language. It's like dancing. So women from different countries produce art with different national characteristics."

Lin Ying was not listening to Qi Jun's hopelessly self-contradictory theories. She was looking at the chaotic smears. And yet, she had the feeling that there was, in fact, a very thin line between those chaotic smears and art: a little bit of rhythm, a hidden dream, something like the moment of sexual orgasm, something that was purely physical sensation yet had the potential to ascend suddenly to a penetrating awareness of the universe.

Hua Hua went to the bathroom to take a shower.

Qi Jun sat on a chair and continued his speech. "Some people say that what we're doing isn't avant-garde art: it's avant-garde but it isn't art. Damn it all, avant-garde in itself is art. It means pulling away from the realm of life ahead of the rest."

Something dripping wet was flung out the half-open bathroom door. It landed with a splat next to the paint can. Qi Jun jumped and stopped talking. It was Hua Hua's leotards, turned inside out as she had peeled them off, with the paint seeping through them as if they were a pitiful mop. Qi Jun tossed back his hair and cast a glance at the bathroom door, now shut. He said to Lin Ying, "The brush is angry. Where was I?"

"You were saying that to be avant-garde you have to want to die." Lin Ying crossed her arms and stood up to lean against the wall.

"Don't turn my words around." Qi Jun waved grandly in the air. "What I mean is, you can't live like a common person. You have to distance yourself from regular daily life, transcend common experience to enter a realm of enlightenment."

Lin Ying pointed to the pile of discarded paper in the bamboo wastebasket on the balcony. "You can't deny that other artists are defeated just by the amount of Xuan paper you use. And your paintbrush, of course, leaves the others in the dust."

Qi Jun made a face as he slapped his hands together and shrugged his shoulders.

"Well, take me, for instance," Lin Ying continued. "I don't know if my poems are considered avant-garde or not."

"Absolutely, much more so than Qi Jun's painting,"

Hua Hua shouted from the bathroom. The shower sounds had stopped and she seemed to be drying herself off.

"I've read your poetry." Qi Jun grabbed a sponge and began cleaning the drips on the floor. "Hua Hua gave me some. Magical. Your disciple salutes you."

"I'm honored." Lin Ying helped him clean as she added, "To me, to be in the avant-garde has nothing to do with severing your relationship with ordinary experience. Instead, it's the result of distillation of life's experience. Experience gets lost in obsessions, but art is enlightenment. The first is about knowledge, the second about wisdom. You get enchantment, obsessions, in things and experiences, but you get enlightenment in reason, through the mind. The enlightenment of art is wild and chaotic and at the same time the highest expression of reason: this is true transcendence."

Hua Hua emerged from the bathroom in a tastefully subdued dressing gown, drying her hair with a striped towel. She threw the towel on a chair and applauded enthusiastically. "Marvelous! Little Lin Ying, since when have you got into Zen?!" She hugged Lin Ying and gave her a big kiss, making her damp in the process. Lin Ying pushed her away.

Qi Jun was disconcerted. He said to Hua Hua, "I didn't know Lin Ying was such a theoretician. I'm ashamed of myself—here I am messing around." He turned to Lin Ying. "Please advise—how do you think I should paint this painting in order to make it truly enlightened?"

Lin Ying was just beginning to answer when the doorbell rang. Qi Jun set down the sponge and turned toward the door. "Look at that, someone comes knocking without even telephoning first. Chinese people have no sense of privacy."

The doorbell rang again. Outside, someone yelled impatiently, "Open up!"

At the sound of the voice Qi Jun's face turned pale. He ran back into the room to turn off the light. "It's my old man," he said. "Don't you two dare come out." With that he pulled the door closed and went out into the hall.

7

The room was plunged into sudden darkness. A street-light across the way lit up the big parasol tree by the balcony, but it was dark in the studio.

"Damn! So secretive!" Hua Hua scolded. "What does he take us for?" She listened for the door to the living room to close, then was quiet.

"Why's he so afraid of his old man?" Lin Ying asked.

"Not just afraid." Hua Hua wrapped the towel around her wet hair, then said in a low voice, "He's old guard, a senior revolutionary, a member of the Central Committee. He was wounded ten times and didn't have children till he was nearly fifty. When Qi Jun gets into trouble, his father fixes it up. When Qi Jun gets into debt, he pays the money. Qi Jun makes sure to stroke him the right way."

Qi Jun now seemed to be explaining something urgently. It was hard to hear what the voices were saying, but the tone of his voice was completely different from normal. His father's, on the other hand, was resonant and deep, and one could decipher snatches of his sentences even though the intervening bedroom muffled much of them. "Truly unspeakable! Look at you, what kind of offspring of a revolutionary military man are you? . . . messing around with these hussies . . ."

"Uh-oh, he's letting loose the cannon." Hua Hua poked Lin Ying in the ribs. "I have to hear this. That old man's sharp, really up on the gossip. I'm afraid this may have something to do with me." She opened the studio door and tiptoed across the bedroom to put her ear against the living-room wall.

"The second and third sons of your Uncle Wang are both at the vice-minister level, the son of your Uncle Yeh is a deputy army commander, Uncle Li's sons are provincial governors . . . all good men, good sons of old heroes. But you? You hang your name on the door of your unit but never go to work. You spend your time mixed up with these damn scoundrels called artists."

Hua Hua had not shut the studio door, and Lin Ying could hear the voices more clearly now. Light seeped in from the hallway, and a light went on in the building across the way, throwing shadows of the tree on the polished floor, gilding it with tawny gold. The timbre of the old man's voice exuded power, carried the unhurried, measured tones of authority.

"Where does the work of the revolution stand in your heart? Where are the people?" The old man had a heavy northern accent. His words sounded heartfelt, as if it would be impossible for him to say anything contrived, and they flowed with practiced ease. "Don't forget, you were born under the red flag, you were raised under the rays of the sun, you lived a privileged life as a result of the sacrifices of countless martyrs.

How many times do I have to say it? What is the Party? The Party is the handful of us!"

Lin Ying could listen no more. The world's most complex political and ethical logic had been reduced by these words to ultimate, clear-cut simplicity. She thought if she sat there another minute, she'd go crazy. The question that had been plaguing her all summer, that she had not until this moment been able to resolve—Why had she been so crazy as to have joined the movement—was now answered plain. It was because she couldn't stand the hypocrisy of the world. The corruption of officials, the way cadres used their position to advance private interests, and so on were secondary. For generations her family had had no contact with either power or money—whoever was getting fat off power, now or later, had little to do with her. But she couldn't stand this kind of harangue covering up what was simply shameless greed. She could not tolerate the hypocrisy. The reason she had refused to listen to Chen Yu's pleas on the night of 3 June was very, very simple: democracy truly flowed in her veins.

She stood up. She spread a large sheet of paper on the floor. She kicked off her shoes and took off her little skirt. She never wore a bra anyway, so after she had taken off her shirt she stood there in only her bikini underpants.

". . . this land under heaven that we've won, naturally we're passing on to our sons!"

Lin Ying paused, then peeled off the underpants and threw them on the pile of clothes. A summer's night breeze floated in the open windows from the balcony, brushing her body. A tremor of excitement flowed from her hot cheeks, down her naked body. She quivered, as if eyes were watching her, as if eyes were looking into her eyes.

"Think about it . . . you should hear the joy in their voices when those other old comrades talk about their sons. But just look at my useless issue! You should feel sorry for me! I'll have to start grooming your older sister's husband. These mountains and rivers, this nation won by the old man, is it all just going to end with you?"

Lin Ying walked over and stood in front of the paint can. In the dim light, she selected two colors, red and black. She picked up a brush and began to paint herself—her face, her arms, her legs. She twisted around to do her back and rear end. The paint was cool and she shivered as she painted her breasts. The brush hairs slithered over her stomach; dribbles of paint rolled down her legs all the way to the cracks between her toes.

My guardian is already in a different world. It's a world so near I can close my eyes and see it and yet so far away that my hands and feet will never reach it, but I still long for it, day after day, using the love I have that nobody needs, using the as-ever, as-before purity of my body and my smeared, feminine heart.

Lin Ying leaned backward carefully to sit down, then slowly uncurled her body until she was lying beside the paper. She closed her eyes; her center was still, unusually transparent; the old man's rumbling words were bringing her inspiration.

I need you, I need you, she was telling herself, because only with you do I belong to this darkness, to this moment in time.

She stretched out her arms, then turned over fiercely, feeling her breasts press down on the paper; she rolled back again and felt her fingers, her hips, her back.

"Madness for these past two months, absolute madness! Fouling up Beijing like this! A twenty-minute trip took me two hours. Demonstrations, roadblocks. How many years do you think it took us to make this nation? Look what it's come to! As though the likes of you really can't hold it together. You're making such trouble for your old man, and doesn't that make them happy, those little bastards and big bastards!"

She felt she was looking down on her own body, seeing it red and black like blood, like sparks, like scars, like ashes. Her brain and her limbs were driven on by her heart. As though fulfilling an eternal promise, she danced her way across the paper.

> But everything that I narrate
> seems to have lost its meaning.
> From the hand you put on me
> I know
> that the sky is still dark.

8

The rain had been pattering outside the window for several hours. Hua Hua had asked her to stay over the evening before, but she had insisted on leaving. She had lain there on the paper for a while before getting up to take a shower, and by the time she put her clothes on and came out into the studio again, Hua Hua and Qi Jun were sitting in the living room talking. The old man had gone, they told her. They thanked her for taking a shower so quietly, for the old man had scolded so vociferously that he wore himself out, and if it hadn't been for his loyal driver, who came up to see how things were getting on and took his arm and helped him get on the elevator to go back downstairs, he might never have left.

Qi Jun called a taxi, and it was dawn when she got home. Unable to sleep, she had scribbled out some lines of poetry. After sleeping a bit, she got up and sat at the table, looking at these lines, wanting to complete them. For example, to add: "a plate, heaped high with the ongoing dream—pain." Too vulgar, she thought.

Hua Hua had borrowed this dormitory room for her from a friend who seldom used it. It was near the hallway entrance and one heard a constant racket of footsteps and doors opening and closing.

Someone knocked. She didn't want to answer but did: it turned out to be someone asking her to come to the telephone.

She heard Hua Hua's voice on the other end of the line before she had a chance to say hello. "Lin Ying, what's going on that it takes you so long?" Without waiting for an answer, Hua Hua went on, "Something's happened! Yan Yan committed suicide. He lay down on the tracks of the Fengtai train. The Public Security Bureau came looking for us early this morning."

Poetry had nothing on the blackness and pain of reality. Lin Ying opened her mouth and found she couldn't speak.

"It happened last night," Hua Hua said.

Last night? Her throat was stopped up by something. It emitted some toneless noises.

"They said there was a diary in his bag, also a book of his poetry."

She saw the train approaching fast and Yan Yan's body stretched out on the tracks, sliced in two by the wheels like a melon. Each side carried with it half a smile; seeds sprayed out in the middle. The train whizzed on, closing on her. The receiver in her hand fell to the ground. Slowly she leaned over to pick it up, and in the earpiece heard Hua Hua's anxious voice, "Lin Ying, where are you? Lin Ying?"

"Here." Lin Ying was suddenly calmer. "Is it possible to see his body?" She wanted to see Yan Yan one last time, no matter what he looked like.

Hua Hua hesitated a moment. "We tried, but the Public Security Bureau wouldn't let us." Yan Yan's notebook had mentioned various matters and implicated various people, and Shao Liuliu had already been called in for interrogation—she just wanted to let Lin Ying know so she could take any necessary measures in time.

"Qi Jun says the Public Security Bureau considers the motive for suicide unclear. They can't understand his notebook, so now they want to say he committed suicide to escape punishment for a crime. But they have no idea what crime it might have been—they're trying to connect it in some way to the disturbance."

The two were silent for a moment. This was a stupid, cruel joke, another fabrication. Lin Ying gripped the receiver tightly, her palm beginning to sweat.

WHEN SHE returned to her room, the first thing she did was to take out her black suitcase and remove from it seven or eight sets of negatives in a manila envelope. The film had been developed long ago, at the end of May, and the prints were in a drawer at Chen Yu's. She hoped he had already disposed of them.

She had thought that there might be a day when she would want more prints, but maybe there would be no need to keep the negatives. She knew Yan Yan's death couldn't implicate her, but she realized many others might be in danger. If the negatives fell into the wrong hands, they could be used as evidence to investigate, even arrest, the people photographed. Naturally, the Security Bureau itself had taken several million photographs already, as well as thousands of feet of video—there must be more than a million people with evidence stored in the files against them.

She interrogated herself intently. The entire process seemed like a play: the square was the stage and this dormitory was also a stage, but the actors were now leaving, one by one. Everything seemed unreal. Where had the error occurred? For there certainly must have been a mistake, a slipup one could point to. Without the movement, Yan Yan would still be writing his poetry, she would still be studying and still living with Chen Yu. Would that life have been more real or even more absurdly empty?

Yan Yan, the only child of a grade-school teacher in a remote country village had passed the exam to study in Beijing University's Chinese department. He was the top candidate from his entire province, and after graduation, he was assigned to teach in the department. But he wasn't a good teacher. Students said his lectures had no real scheme or train of thought.

But she and Yan Yan had a lot in common, especially in their appreciation of the subject of death. She thought of Yan Yan's poetry, the melancholy aura that could break your heart, that crept over her own emotions like moss. She remembered especially a strange entreaty—"Please allow me to accomplish one last tragic event." Her heart had tightened every time she read that line.

And then in the winter, Douzi, Yan Yan's wife, had killed herself. Yan Yan had used liquor, cigarettes, nights roaming the streets, to deaden his pain—she and Hua Hua had worried that he might try to commit suicide himself, but when the demonstrations started in the spring, committing suicide because of your own problems became a little ridiculous. Insanely, Yan Yan joined the hunger strike: most others had eaten as much as possible before going to the square, but Yan Yan went with an empty stomach, fasted until he fainted, and twice had to be sent to the hospital. As soon as he was on his feet he ran back to the square. In the end his fasting had given him bleeding ulcers, and he was in the hospital when he might have been awaiting death at the square. Yesterday evening, he had completed the action of dividing a being already split in two. What he did was predictable: ending a life that had lost all significance was, in the end, not so much a death as the birth of a real achievement.

Perhaps it really was time for her to start thinking about how to live.

Do I have that kind of courage? she asked herself. My generation was born to enact a tragedy. We came into the world in the 1960s, when tens of millions of people were dying of famine; we were not the fruit of desire but the instinctive reaction of the human race to replace itself after a catastrophe. Then came the Cultural Revolution; under the brilliant glare of the shining Red Sun we grew up pale and thin, hiding in dark, gray corners. Our youth was spent in the emptiness attendant upon a loss of faith, in ferocious attention to all kinds of hope, but when we wanted to cash in on them we discovered that the world is not built on hope alone. So the first half of our lives has been a series of self-contradictions. If there's going to be a second half, it can only mean drifting along from day to day, resigned to circumstances, competing to be good at feigning ignorance.

Lin Ying picked up the negatives and looked at them against the light from the window.

Among slabs of green one could see the darkness of human figures. The black patches with long red lines were army tanks. The contorted black bodies were perhaps the fasting students. The twisting green triangles were perhaps pennants. As she surveyed the images, she cut them to shreds with her scissors.

"Have you seen the two readers' letters criticizing Yan Yan in the *Poetry Gazette*?" Hua Hua had been so angry on the phone her voice was trembling. "They said he was a literary failure. There's only this kind of cooked-up criticism right now. It's such a cowardly shame."

"The bullets are getting closer."

"What did you say?" Hua Hua hadn't heard her.

"I said it's just a matter of time now," said Lin Ying.

One after another friend was being written off by the pen writing the great book of truth. The world had become shockingly unfamiliar. I shouldn't have run that night, shouldn't have hidden. I should have lain down in the middle of the street. Too few, not too *many*, Chinese poets commit suicide.

This is a crazy century, a train that has jumped its tracks and run amok. The more its passengers have been tossed around, the more dangerous it has become. Synchronizing their movements further would lead to mass calamity. If each person could decide his own way of doing things, choose the most appropriate methods for himself, perhaps we could bring the train back on track.

I'm not the only one; we are not the only ones. Since the beginning of this century every new generation, hot blood pounding in its veins, has wanted to do something. With what result? When have its attempts not ended with all the pots smashed? Every time there has been hardship, loss of life, bloodshed; each attempt has simply caused China to move backward.

If we truly go beyond the limit, it will be because we are too inclined toward collective action.

Lin Ying kept on with her scissors. She pulled open a roll of film that was all dark gray—it had been exposed before being used. She put down her scissors and collected all the fragments of film and negatives into a paper funnel, then went to the lavatory in the corridor and poured them into the latrine. She watched the water gurgle as it swirled downward, until there was only foam in the basin.

4

1

It was too peaceful this evening. Unnaturally peaceful.

Yesterday was Army Day, guards everywhere, soldiers marching around with rifles at the ready. Additional sentry posts were added to the main roads. Rumor had it that the watermelons prepared for the army had been secretly injected with poison; this only made the soldiers more jumpy and on guard. Pedestrians hurried by expressionless, for either gladness or sadness could lead to interrogation. When Hua Hua asked Lin Ying to go out with her, she said it was best not to wear anything completely white or completely black or half white, half black.

"You can't even be in mourning if someone in your family's died. Best to wear the gaudiest thing possible, so let's dress up!" She wore a tight-fitting matching top and skirt with light yellow flowers against a deep red background.

Lin Ying found a dress that revealed her shoulders, white flowers against pale red. She brushed her hair back and tied it tightly at the back of her head. When she saw in the mirror how pale her lips were she smeared on two thin lines of lipstick. Then she tied a narrow, transparent white scarf around her neck. She looked once more in the mirror, picked up her purse, and went out the door with Hua Hua.

Two days earlier, just after dinner, Li Jiangjiang had come looking for Lin Ying to tell her that the visa for Germany had arrived. He would soon be leaving for Heidelberg—university classes didn't start until October, so in fact he didn't really have to go immediately. He was excited, in a completely different frame of mind from the grief-stricken state he'd been in when he came back from Changchun and heard the news about Yan Yan.

The two of them had gone for a walk.

"Don't you want me to stay on here a few more days?" he had asked.

His entreating tone made Lin Ying nod her head. "Of course. Nothing would be better."

The branch of a tree was suspended over them, the moon hanging on the end of it like a great white hollow. Cicadas chirped in the bushes with thin, shrill voices; when anyone approached they would stop, move away, and then start up again. A distant streetlight shone pale yellow and fuzzy, as if through fog.

She walked beside Li Jiangjiang. Under the lights their shadows moved to overlap, then part.

"When are you going with me? When are you going with me?" The hoarse sound of a man singing from a window in Building B gave the popular tune an unusually plaintive tone.

"That bum again!" Li Jiangjiang raised his head. The singer, whom he knew, could not get his PhD dissertation accepted. His adviser had been a progressive, a self-professed critic of Marxism who had once been magnanimously tolerant of the "new theories" but who had returned to orthodoxy and been promoted to deputy director of the institute with the recent tide of repression in intellectual circles. Now he vigorously attacked anything heretical. The student couldn't keep up with his adviser's shifting positions; the adviser turned against him and accused him of "mistakes in his ideological position." People said the student was no longer quite right in the head, that perhaps at the beginning he had pretended to be crazy so as to let off steam, but now he truly was.

"I wanted to give you my hopes and my freedom. All you did was laugh at me for having nothing at all, oh, nothing at all."

They walked by the library, putting Building B far behind them, but snatches of the song still came floating through the air.

Li Jiangjiang stopped. "There's something . . . I don't know if I should tell you or not . . . it has to do with you."

"Don't worry, I've heard plenty of rumors about me."

Li Jiangjiang nodded. "You know of course that women poets are always a target of criticism—you hear a lot of rumors about them in general. But none about yourself."

"Quite the opposite! I often hear what's said about me. Lots of people seem to want to tell me things of their own accord. As for others, I can imagine. Whatever else, it's bound to be irregular, unclean, impure!"

Li Jiangjiang denied this. "I don't believe those vulgar people who gossip. And I understand about the entanglement with Chen Yu."

"But you don't want to hear about any of my relations with other men?"

"I'm just worried about you."

"Worried about what?"

Li Jiangjiang didn't answer. "I just hope everything will go well for you. Fine. Let's not talk about it. I've never met such a stubborn woman! And you're almost thirty years old."

"Oh, so you worry how I'll come out in the great matter of marriage." Lin Ying spoke for him. "You're worried that with my reputation nobody will dare ask me—dare to be seen with a woman of such ill repute. Imagine, you were even so generous as to want to help take her abroad." She grew angrier as she spoke. "You feel you have this great compassion, saving a woman from prostitution. Like some noble operatic character."

Li Jiangjiang stared at her, amazed, as though he scarcely recognized her. "Don't be so harsh. Women can manage to defend themselves against smears."

"Those women are slaves!" She knew she shouldn't get angry, but at this particular moment the idea of making a woman discipline herself made her furious. "So-called fallen women are just the ones who recognize that women must be masters of their fate. They are the most superior women in any generation. You should respect them!"

"You're going to extremes!"

These past two months the change in Lin Ying had been considerable. He could understand it—she was facing difficulties and setbacks that were almost more than a woman could bear. At the same time, he could not accept the way she turned around everything he said.

They reached the red brick wall of the compound; they could hear the roar of the traffic just outside. Lin Ying reached up and snapped off a branch and threw it on the ground. "All right, I'll tell you my extreme." She spoke very calmly. "I'll tell you: women who take the initiative with men are the only ones who truly understand the pleasures of sex, the only ones who can write poetry about sex. Don't be so surprised; I'm one of those women."

"I'd like to see just how you 'take the initiative,' " Li Jiangjiang retorted.

"I'll show you," she flung at him. Li Jiangjiang was still agitated and didn't understand what she had just said, but she did and blushed.

Part of her own shadow was cast on the wall, part on the ground. She moved closer to the wall, to make the shadow stand straighter, not look so uncomfortably crooked. With her back to Li Jiangjiang now, she told him that she had wanted to give him a present on his departure—it shouldn't be hard to guess what it would have been. Now there didn't seem to be any need.

Li Jiangjiang sat down on the grass. "When I got to

Germany, the first thing I planned to do was find a way to get you out of China."

"Well then, I've spoiled your kindness and saved you the trouble." Seeing how upset he was, she softened her tone. "I'm trying to think of how to send you off —don't spoil my fun."

Li Jiangjiang, at a loss for words, realized that he had somehow overreacted.

"Let's part on good terms," she said, "so you'll never forget me."

He perked up and started talking about how he hoped she'd think about going abroad anyway, even if not to Germany.

Lin Ying shook her head. Outside China, her future would be a matter of waiting on tables, cleaning houses, or babysitting. If it came to that, all women might begin to think that being a "flowerpot" for men was not such an unfortunate life after all. Struggling to eke out a living outside China might make poetry not only something of minor significance but even an affectation and encumbrance.

And inside China? Poetry's time was over. She knew that. Her poetic style, with its complex metaphors and suggestiveness, expressed a vast, unspeakable wound, a voluntary withdrawal, a reluctance to converse with actuality. The number of journals willing to publish her poetry was already pitifully small and would soon be zero. Her poems would appear only in mimeographed journals. Being a professional poet in China was nothing but a dream.

She sat down beside Li Jiangjiang. Her hand lightly smoothed his hair, then rested on his shoulder. "I hope you'll find a nice girl for a wife."

"You're the most unfathomable woman I know." His hands brushed over the grass before him and he didn't raise his head to look at her.

It would be good if the two of them would truly miss each other, even if only for a moment. Any longer, and the promises made would become bonds. She wanted to tell him this, to make him feel better. Instead, she suddenly found herself blurting, "But, I hereby declare: What I want to do is not for you, it's for myself."

2

The next day Lin Ying had just finished eating lunch when she got a telephone call from Wu Wei.

"Know what the latest is on Chen Yu? He's confessed to all the charges."

"What exactly were the charges?"

"All kinds. He's admitted his guilt."

"What you mean is that he's confessed to being a counterrevolutionary, confessed to sleeping with two women at the same time and said I'm one of the two?"

"Don't shout," Wu Wei said with alarm. "I'm calling you for your own good, to let you get ready."

"Ready for what? They're coming to arrest me?"

"I don't know."

Lin Ying thanked him, politely and formally, then put down the telephone.

Chen Yu was not a superman. This era did not need supermen. The only heroes you would find putting up a heroic resistance in prison were actors in Communist operas. She could understand his confessing. What she couldn't bear was the vagueness of the charges. All these political and ethical accusations were unclear, their definitions uncertain—therefore all the more powerful as a means of controlling people, of keeping them from any sense of security and getting them to confess to crimes and to surrender.

She walked slowly back to her borrowed room. She had wanted to visit Chen Yu but hadn't been able to find out where he was locked up. Visitors were not being allowed to pay calls on any serious cases relating to 4 June.

When Chen Yu had tried to explain himself on the telephone that evening, he had said that Mei Ling had been shocked, had needed his comfort. If that was true she could, and in fact should, see things from their perspective. Her reaction not only had been unnecessary but had damaged both her and Chen Yu. She could even make herself understand Chen Yu's ambivalence, forgive his equivocation between two women.

She rubbed her face, wet with perspiration. She went to the lavatory, poured a basin of cold water, and scrubbed her face with a washcloth. If she had thought as clearly that early morning as she did today and if Chen Yu and Mei Ling had felt the same way, she should have been willing to play out this accusation of so-called indecent behavior—to cast off all self-imposed restraints, sleep with them in the same bed, make love in the same bed, each comforting the others. They would, perhaps, still be comforting one another today, she would not be so frightened and confused, her mind would not be such a terrifying blank. How easily people allow their prejudices to destroy them.

Instead, they had been forced to expose, and inform on, one another, destroy one another. If Mei Ling had accused Chen Yu in order to take revenge for his being with her and if Chen Yu had admitted to the fabricated charge and implicated her in order to pay her back for being with Li Jiangjiang, then she had brought this retribution on herself in her intolerance. The chain of events would be due to her having accepted the conventional standards of this wretched world.

And then there was Wu Wei! How was it he had never given her a chance even to catch her breath? His concern might be genuine, but it might also be pretense. She had the feeling he was rather glad to be throwing stones into the well, once he saw that Chen Yu had fallen in. Maybe he hadn't sunk so far as to be an informer, but at the very least he had a tyrannical streak and loved to torment people.

Lin Ying hung her towel on the rack and gave the open door a kick as she left so that it closed with a bang. Headfirst, she plunged onto the bed, her red skirt billowing up over her like a flame. The dark curtains blocked out most of the light—they were navy blue, inscribed with darker characters the color of soy sauce, declaring inanely stupid notions like "good fortune" and "happiness." This separation from the searing brilliance of the day outside made her burning body feel even more solitary.

Lying on her side, she caressed herself, the smooth hardness of her body merging into the soft erectness of her breasts. She tossed her loose hair and turned on her back to look at the ceiling. She had never before felt such a strong need for self-pity, though from the time she had first caught sight of her reflection in the river, loving herself was one of the means she always used to lessen suffering.

I always yield to gentleness. My body has a strange

odor, the same as the bullets that day. I want to stay like this, not caring about my own purity, not caring about being mindlessly loyal. I don't want to worry anymore about your changes of heart.

Images from the past came pressing in on her; new wounds now took on color, like a sunrise. And if I were to stay like this, would this city, which never stooped to smile at me before, would it open its arms to me?

She felt as though she were standing on top of a high tower. From inside came the continuous booming of a great bell, its vibrations reverberating in and out of her body. Men were merely notes in the sweep of the music, no one man sufficient to make a tune but together capable of an unforgettable melody, music that ought, ideally, to lead her to abandon. If only she could play on them as she wished.

Time is measured in changes. In this brief space of my lifetime, changes are coming faster and faster and time is stretching out in equal measure. Why not welcome this? The more the better, especially men, and we can appreciate the differences in the quality of the music. Why not?

What am I thinking about? she asked herself in amazement.

You're simply oversexed!

And yet what woman has not sought oblivion in the same way, her head full of indecent thoughts? What woman dares to admit this, even to herself, admit that she has this kind of lust—like hunger, like thirst? All of us yearn for variety, for whatever will lift us above the tribulations of the world.

Yes, and who doesn't do these things in her dreams? She could at least answer for herself. And don't we immerse our minds in erotic thoughts? In real life we walk a tightrope, trying to maintain balance. On the one side are the things we must know; on the other, things we can't know. On one side are permitted experiences; on the other, experiences we ache for and dream of. How many times do thoughts of sex push us to the precipice? We tremble, we're afraid, we dare not take another step. We're even scared of looking around to see clearly.

Lust may be a kind of poison that destroys our lives. But the minute you understand that life, by its nature, is going to end anyway, the poison turns from a dangerous temptation to the promise of rebirth.

Why not lift the glass, then, and drink?

THE NATIONAL Education Commission put out an official document canceling the writing program. Instead, they turned it into a series of short-term courses on Marxism and Leninism, for which students were to be selected from local cultural units. China's newly appointed head of cultural affairs said that the nation should not spend money cultivating degenerate writers who could write nothing but trash that people didn't want to read and couldn't understand. The graduate-level course was dropped without mention, dying without even having time to be sick.

Lin Ying had been aware from the start that she was waiting in vain. And now her only reason for staying in Beijing had disappeared. But her second sister had written advising her not to come back home. Once she returned to her old unit it would be hard to explain what she'd been doing during the disturbance. The security apparatus in a small place had fewer targets of scrutiny—and focused particularly on students returning from Beijing, whom they kept under intense surveillance. Things that would not be regarded as worth noting in Beijing were major cases in the local arena.

Her sister had taken the obligatory presents and gone to visit the "responsible person" in her old factory. He had told her that Lin Ying could only extend her leave of absence for another six months, after which she'd be treated as though she had voluntarily quit. The supervisor told her it would be best for Lin Ying not to show up for a while—if she weren't around, they could keep up the pretense that she was still in school, still furthering her education.

Lin Ying did not know where she could go now. Chen Yu and Li Jiangjiang could no longer provide even a temporary roof. Would she have to find another man in order to have a place to live? She felt that she was moving in a direction that had been preordained. Her destination, already visible, was calling her forward.

When she was small, she often sat at the top of their narrow stairs, the sounds of horns blowing up from the river, a light mist in the air. Her mother and father would be arguing loudly inside, sometimes physically fighting. They had so many things to fight about—grievances, problems too tangled to unravel. Her father would barrel out the door, furious, and Lin Ying would dart to one side as he charged down the stairs. Seeing her, he would yell, "I'll kill you!" then go on without stopping.

She didn't know whom her father wanted to kill, but he was yelling at her when he said this. His face would be red, as though he really were ready for murder. Trembling, she would wait for the blow. She knew her father loathed her existence—so many daughters at home, and she was the eldest, the first disappointment.

She would never forget the time her father had made for the door and she didn't have time to hide. He had slapped her across the face so hard that she fell against the stairs, blood flowing from her mouth. Her father came over, picked her up in his arms, and carried her back into their room, softly and gently cradling her.

She said to herself, Father, you brought me into this world. You gave me a tough life but also tenacity: the body of a woman but a stubborn mind. Right now, I desperately need you to hit me again: hit me a hard one, a real blow.

3

Li Jiangjiang's going-away party was held in Qi Jun's suite of rooms at Forest Slope. There was plenty of room, and the apartment was in the middle of a high-cadre district and so wouldn't attract too much police attention. Li Jiangjiang had some business to do during the day, so he came by himself. Lin Ying and Hua Hua came by later—they had to take several different buses—arriving when it was already beginning to get dark. A number of people were talking in the living room, many of them former members of the Degraded Survivors' Club who had stayed on in Beijing.

A woman standing beside Nan An had such close-cropped hair she looked almost bald. Her face was heavily painted, her fake eyelashes long and black. Lin Ying recognized her as Xiao Hong, a Voidist poet. Lin Ying hadn't known that her poetics extended all the way to her hair. And there were other women whom she had never seen before. Shao Liuliu, wearing an evening gown with a very low neckline and long dangling earrings, stood in the middle of a circle of admiring men. Hua Hua and Lin Ying detoured around some cartons of beer in the hall and went into the studio. Li Jiangjiang and Yan Heituo quickly greeted them.

Where had Qi Jun gone, Hua Hua wanted to know. Yan Heituo said he'd gone to get a painting that he had asked someone to mount for him, but he would be right back. "He sure cuts it close," said Hua Hua.

Li Jiangjiang pulled Lin Ying aside. "See," he said, "everyone seems to think I'm really going!"

"And I'm the only one not being sentimental about this last evening, right? My dear," Lin Ying said, "how do you want me to demonstrate my reluctance to part from you?"

Li Jiangjiang had never heard her call him "dear" before, and he knew she was teasing. In fact, she had seldom been in such a good mood. "I've never seen you drunk," he said. "Tonight, how about getting a little tipsy for me?"

Lin Ying took the beer he handed her and, in the same jocular tone, said, "My poor child, what kind of thing is that for a man to say?" She suddenly felt a lump in her throat and her eyes blurred as she turned away.

Wu Wei's voice came from the doorway—the living room was becoming too crowded and people were moving into the studio. "By nature," he was saying, "Chinese people are weak but rebellious. Japanese, on the other hand, are tough by nature but obedient. Chinese are yang on the outside, yin on the inside. Japanese are yin on the outside, yang on the inside. That's why

China is poor and Japan is rich." This was the great discovery of his work in comparative cultural studies. He said that lately he'd been thinking of writing an article on his insights, that some Japanese scholars had already expressed great interest.

Shao Liuliu yawned, covering her mouth with her hand. This seemed to dampen Wu Wei's enthusiasm and he stopped talking. She said quickly, "Very interesting, really very interesting. Tell us more. These grand, sweeping theories really open my eyes." She raised her eyebrows and opened her eyes wide. "Sometimes even my mouth!" She pointed to her sexy wide-open lips. Everyone laughed.

Behind Wu Wei sat a woman with shoulder-length hair, dressed in an olive-colored dress buttoned to the neck. You knew at a glance from that dress that this was Su Jie, Wu Wei's wife. Lin Ying had never met her—she wasn't a writer—but her name was often heard in Beijing literary circles. She only had to get a whiff that Wu Wei liked someone and she'd go right to work—make friends with the woman and promise to help her in whatever way she could, so that the other woman could not help being grateful for the attention. Either the woman's chagrin would destroy any budding feelings she might have for Wu Wei or she would surrender to the wife's persistence, just to avoid having her come around all the time uninvited.

Su Jie's abiding principle was never to say bad things about Wu Wei to anyone in public. Even before a possible rival, she would praise her husband to the skies. She knew that her future lay with Wu Wei.

Su Jie had once called Lin Ying. She had hemmed

and hawed and finally asked if Lin Ying had seen Wu Wei recently.

"Oh yes, we see each other often. We're quite good friends." Lin Ying had made things very clear.

"Is that so?" Su Jie had not expected this. She quickly changed the subject. "Have you head the rumors going around about you?"

"Yes, I know them all," Lin Ying had said. "Have you heard the rumors going around about you?"

"What rumors could there possibly be about me?"

"That you're about to lose control of your husband!"

Su Jie had been shocked into silence. After a moment, she changed the subject again. "Our son is so smart. He'll be going to a top elementary school soon. You know what he said to his father yesterday? So clever!"

Lin Ying's stomach had turned at this. The woman on the line was an extremely clever adversary—speaking of their son was a brilliant move. "Excuse me," she was going to say. There was no reason to torment this woman. But the reflexes at the other end of the line were faster than her own: Su Jie was the first to say, "I'm so sorry, I've wasted your precious time. I hope we'll have another nice chat sometime soon." Upon which she had hung up.

The image in Lin Ying's mind was of a pitiful plain woman fretting all day about how to keep her husband. Now when she saw Su Jie she was astounded. Compared to Wu Wei, Su Jie was truly good-looking. She was poised, knew just where to put her hands and feet. And she had a very effective smile that she could hold for an exceedingly long time. "In the kitchen, in the drawing room, she's good for both," Lin Ying remembered Wu Wei bragging once about his wife.

For once Wu Wei did not come over to talk to Lin Ying about Chen Yu, held back perhaps by his wife's presence. He lifted his glass at her across the room and she nodded in return. Su Jie glanced over and smiled a perfectly modulated smile. Lin Ying nodded at her, too. She had no desire to know this woman, and by the looks of it the feeling was mutual. Wu Wei didn't introduce them, so they were saved from an empty, conventional exchange.

4

An old Cultural Revolution song was being played on the sound system:

> The sun is most crimson,
> Chairman Mao is most kind,
> Your glorious thought forever
> On my soul will shine.

The lyrics were popular again among Beijing students and artists but by now the style of the tune was completely different, a crooning style like in a 1930s Shanghai dance hall, soft and lingering, that made you feel limp. The instrumental accompaniment, on the other hand, beat out a heavy rhythm, as though the singer were in a daze, eyes half closed. People smiled and started humming whenever they heard the new version.

Qi Jun's sound system—it had been in the living room and he probably had moved it into the studio just for this party—was the highest quality of any in Beijing, his amplifiers Sony, the loudspeaker Kano, the tape deck Matsushita. Qi Jun often turned out the light to enjoy the range of his equipment. "If I could get by without using little Japs' stuff," he said, "I would. I inherited my anti-Japanese attitude from my father. But I can't get by without using their stuff, so I do."

> Higher than the sky is your munificence,
> Deeper than the ocean is your beneficence,
> The sun in our hearts will never go down.
> You are our savior, our shining star.

"Take that thing off!" someone called. "You think it's so clever, violating the sacred man. Don't you know he's just sitting up there all happy, thinking, Sing it however you want, the words still speak for my holiness."

Yan Heituo stopped the song and put in another tape, this time of classical music.

Someone asking for details about Yan Yan's suicide was quickly silenced. "Don't bring it up, it'll destroy the mood. What's more, his lover's here tonight . . ." Then there were urgent questions about who his lover was. On the other side of the room, people were debating intellectual movements. Wu Wei said that in the 1980s the Chinese intellectuals had been in lockstep, everyone favoring a monolithic kind of holism for the sake of all, and thinking they alone were right; the result was a refusal to compromise and eventually direct conflict. Nan An patted Wu Wei on the shoulder, saying, "You're not too bad, you rascal. You've found someone to blame!"

The fucking osteoporosis is showing up again in these Chinese literary types, Lin Yin thought bitterly. Only two months, and the spine-bending self-penitence had already begun. Before another two years go by they'll all be adhering to Party policy. Hell, another few years and they'll be kneeling down in front of whoever holds power!

It was already nine o'clock. The evening air was heavy, pressing down on Beijing's feeble streetlights. There was no breeze to disperse the heat, and it felt as though it might rain.

Yan Heituo clapped his hands and announced in a loud voice, "Attention, everyone! Quiet a moment, please. The master of the house is out. My humble person is usurping this occasion to represent him as master of ceremonies. Riding on the east wind, after the illustrious occasion yesterday of the sixtieth birthday of our People's Army, we are holding this going-away party for our esteemed theoretician, Li Jiangjiang. Now I would like to entertain toasts."

Wu Wei was the first to lift his glass. "Here's to an Eastern mind for the head of German philosophy!" he shouted.

Li Jiangjiang was still looking very much the student, with denim jeans bleached almost white, a tucked-in white shirt, sneakers. He smiled, a little embarrassed. "Truth has no nationality," he said.

"In the end," Nan An went on, "the ruthless rationalism of Western thought will just have to submit to the hard-core irrationality of Chinese."

"I prefer 'of the Chinese,'" Shao Liuliu cut in. Everyone was blank for a moment, then laughed.

Li Jiangjiang began to loosen up, for the genial mood was getting to him. In the midst of the laughter he drawled, with perfect timing, "Wisdom hides under every kind of hair."

Everyone was amused, and Shao Liuliu doubled up with laughter.

Two years before, the Degraded Survivors had toasted "subjectivity" every time they got together for a party. The tradition in making toasts was to exaggerate to the point of inappropriateness, to ridicule fervently. The person being toasted had to be especially sharp to respond without falling into a verbal trap. If the words touched on dangerous subjects, so much the better, but they had to be oblique, not blatant; the witticisms had to have double meanings. It was said that those who practiced this kind of verbal gamesmanship were far better at it than the ancients had ever been: contemporary political movements and battles had honed their skills. Hoping to surpass the ladies' banquet in *Dream of the Red Chamber*, they particularly favored women's witticisms. Remarks were considered voluntary, but remaining silent was felt to be very poor form. These self-important literary figures were unwilling to concede to anyone at an event like this.

But this sort of gathering hadn't been held in 1989. At the start of the year, it had been impossible—you simply couldn't find the people—and later it was impossible and nobody was in the mood. This was the first time the group had braved it, taken advantage of the chance to vent frustrations and restore good spirits, not just hold a literary gathering.

Hua Hua now declared, "I hope Jiangjiang will pay the Germans back for their participation in the eight-power Allied forces' occupation of Beijing in 1900. He should take some blond celebrity—"

Li Jiangjiang interrupted her: "Cleansing the national shame is our collective responsibility. I will do my humble part and charge ahead."

Shouts of "Hear! Hear!" and proposals to drink up.

"Best marry a blond," added Shao Liuliu. "The east wind will triumph over the west wind."

"I haven't finished . . . and raise a nest of black-haired, blue-eyed bastards . . . to improve both the inferior and the superior races." Li Jiangjiang's nonsense was unimpeded.

Lin Ying didn't need others looking at her to know that everyone was waiting to hear what Li Jiangjiang's girlfriend, or former girlfriend, had to say. She hadn't wanted to join in the banter that hid the peculiar Chinese need to feel important, which she suspected was behind all the jokes. "The world is revolving downward," she said now.

She looked at Li Jiangjiang and said to him softly, "A solitary rider, body all sweaty, grits his teeth and rides into the last rays of the setting sun."

Li Jiangjiang picked up his glass.

Lin Ying said, "Close your eyes. Imagine the scene."

Li Jiangjiang actually did close his eyes. "Are you trying to persuade me that action is not as good as staying still?"

"I'm not exhorting you."

"I understand," Li Jiangjiang said. "All right. At the end the prodigal son comes home."

"Getting closer," she said. "Redemption is beyond; when everything's scraped clean, life begins."

Li Jiangjiang smiled. "Damn, that's a most interesting world."

So the two of them went back and forth with the Zen koans, neither giving in to the other. Yan Heituo finally said, "Distinguished gentleman, distinguished lady, please set a date to continue cutting each other to pieces. Today the two of you come out equal."

Lin Ying was puzzled. Li Jiangjiang was supposed to have read so many books, and yet he didn't understand what she meant. Perhaps they were already thinking differently. She had meant that no matter how hard you try, facing east or west, and no matter what you seek, in the end you have to come back to yourself. You can't escape to another world.

Yan Heituo was saying, "I'm preparing a program especially for Li Jiangjiang, as a prize for his verbal battle against such wit."

5

The clapping continued for minutes, then weakened and suddenly stopped. Out of the silence came the sound of a bamboo flute and a zither, first one, then the other. The music seemed transparent, with no melody. Then the Chinese two-string fiddle slowly joined in, not covering the flute but suddenly calling higher and higher, like the lament in a Sichuan opera when the grieving dead soul calls from a mountaintop. Just when the pitch could no longer be sustained, the cry and the instruments receded like a tide to silence. Soft and deep came the sound of a great Chinese drum. The throbbing was first heavy and measured, then lighter and farther away. A woman's voice calmly began reading:

> It was a full, ripe seed that was covered by a red shadow.
> Now, see which of us is more willing to make a deal,
> Whose juices move more slowly, sluggishly,
> Whose face is more easily distorted.
> Frost and cold hide at dawn, insects hide at dusk.
> After we are disposed of, only that seed will go on,
> Because of us,
> Implacably growing

The taped voice was without artifice, without excessive emotion. At first, it sounded flat, but gradually, out of the flow of the words unfolded their meaning:

> Your eyes are telling me,
> Well, compare a knife to a knife, then, no analogic knife.
> Putting us together ends me, like ice crystals on a fire.
> Happiness is what it is. Let what's happened be a preface:
>   The
> Sharp cry of an introduction to this time, next place

The sound of the fiddle took the place of the poem, once again pulling together visions that had been ripped apart. A strange beauty, a familiar ache, all the regrets that could not be assuaged—Lin Ying could scarcely recognize the poetry. She had accepted Yan Heituo's request and given him some of her most recent unpublished poems, and he had said that he would do a little editing when he set it to music. Hearing it like this, she felt her poem had gained new meanings, hard to capture on a sheet of paper, and the tenderness of her original work had been diluted.

Hands folded, Li Jiangjiang leaned against the wall, mesmerized. Naturally he believed the poem had been composed for him. He was the only one there who had read any of Lin Ying's recent work.

> I am not a flowerbud, the first opening of a bud . . .
> What fell into your embrace was yesterday's fruit

His expression suddenly changed. Lin Ying realized he might be reading a different meaning into these two lines: that his old debt could not be forgotten. It's just a poem! Lin Ying wanted to shout at him. A critic should know that! Poetry is not a postcard!

But then again, perhaps he's right. I am the one who has spoken, and I am also the one who hasn't said anything. Certain things do not go into poetry. I was the one who came from a wooden house on stilts by the river, who wove a life into hard fiber lines. They are all me.

Li Jiangjiang moved around the sofa and went out through the glass door onto the balcony.

She remembered the banner that the students in the writing program had waved during the demonstration: "Long Live Understanding!"

What stupidity! Did it mean that whoever says he understands should enjoy "a long, long life"?

No. I will never depend on someone else's understanding to live my life. What will I become? A slave who behaves according to the kind grace of others? No, please, I would rather have misunderstanding. I am made of misunderstandings!

Breathing heavily, Qi Jun strode in with a long rolled-up painting under his arm. He put it down to pick up a glass of wine, which he drained. "Sorry! Very sorry!" he shouted. "Making you wait all this time! It's too damn hot!"

Yan Heituo was fiddling with the tapes, pretending he hadn't seen Li Jiangjiang's embarrassment. But even before the music ended, people had split up into little groups to talk. Yan Heituo was enthusiastically discussing techniques of electronic mixing. When Qi Jun came in, he said, "Excellent. Ladies and gentlemen, attention please. We are now ready for the main event of the evening."

Qi Jun pointed to the rolled-up painting. "I guarantee this will cure homesickness for anyone going abroad."

He adjusted the large black frames on his nose, then pretended to survey the wall next to the door. He asked those leaning against it to move aside, then rubbed it a little with his hands, though the wall was already clean. He had the habit of arranging everything in a room to the last detail: he got a bamboo picture hanger from across the hall, undid the silk ribbon around the painting, and hooked the bamboo rod into the loop on top. The painting slowly unwound as he lifted the top of it to the ceiling, where two hooks hung.

Everyone stood in amazement. Nobody said a word.

It was an extremely large work mounted on patterned silk. The background paper—four or five feet wide, and six or seven feet high—had been covered almost entirely with paint, but in a few places a pale gray showed through. Linked red splashes intermingled with traces of black ink. In places water had washed the colors, so that the various layers of red and black overlapped; in other places one could see the dry astringency of brush strokes. The alternation of thick and thin formed a wild rhythm of tonal shades. The effect was staggering, but it was impossible to say what the painting was.

Lin Ying was dumbstruck. She guessed from the red and black that this was the sheet of paper that she herself had painted that night. She didn't know whether Hua Hua had seen the painting on the floor; after all, the next morning there had been the news of Yan Yan's suicide, which put them all in a panic. It was fortunate that Lin Ying had not stayed that night, or she might have had another hard-to-explain detail for the security police. It looked as though it was Qi Jun who had found the paper, and evidently he had immediately understood it. Without saying a word, he had added a few touches of his own.

Lin Ying had to admit that Qi Jun had an uncommonly good eye. He had grasped the emotional meaning and emphasized its latent rhythm. The result, so deftly capitalizing on the capacity of the paper to absorb water, made the composition fly. Random dots of color—some pure green, some light yellow, some mixed—enlivened the more austere red and black. Had Qi Jun done this intentionally, or had there been paint left on the floor? The dots sprang out of the background alarmingly, exploding in the darkness.

She discovered that everyone in the room was slowly moving backward to assess the painting from a distance. Lin Ying retreated until she could clearly see her own form in it. At the same moment she saw Hua Hua open her mouth in shock. Hua Hua was realizing how the painting had been made, but she didn't know which woman Qi Jun had used as a brush. No doubt she also recognized that it had been painted by a completely naked body, for the results were different from the painting she had done in her leotards. The fabric had retained water, so the contours of the colored blotches changed more: the modulations of ink tone from the naked body were more distinct, the contours more discernible, and the overall rhythms of the painting more natural.

Qi Jun stood at the side of the painting, first looking out at this most critical of audiences, then looking back at his masterpiece. Pleased with himself, he tapped one foot lightly on the glossy floor.

"I see it." Li Jiangjiang was the first to speak.

Qi Jun asked, "What do you see?"

"I see what you're trying to express here. You want to show the power of the artistic imagination, how it uses its own dynamics to unfold naturally, even under conditions of random chaos."

"I confess," said Qi Jun, his eyes finding Lin Ying in the crowd and smiling toward her, "I confess you are a professional and so have understood it."

"Quit being so abstruse!" yelled Nan An, rudely interrupting them. "I can see myself what's going on here."

"And I can see what painted it," Yan Heituo put in, excited. "My God, this is fucking brilliant!"

They charged forward, each trying to show everyone else how to read the disorderly jumble of colors. At first people were skeptical, then the number of converts grew, and soon there was an excited hubbub.

Qi Jun kept saying that imagining things like this was too absurd, that it was like a Rorschach test—you think what you want into a painting and soon it exhibits your idea back at you. But the more he refuted Nan An and Yan Heituo, the more firmly people believed them. Nan An pointed to several places that showed without doubt, he said, the contours of a rear end pressing down; you could see the crack between the buttocks. And this was the movement of the breasts, with the impression of a nipple. And here was the line between shoulder and armpit, here was the opening between the legs, here was the triangular patch below the stomach and so on. "It has to be two men holding a naked woman over the paper and turning her around to create this," Nan An concluded, categorically.

Yan Heituo said this kind of thing had been done by Westerners, that for Easterners to do it later was to harm the general principle of their national pride. Being second these days led to nothing but failure. But then he couldn't help laughing: in the end, a good painting was a good painting. How was it that when this group got together they endlessly compared East and West? they left no room for appreciating art pure and simple.

Su Jie was very disturbed, and she took it out on Qi Jun. If what everyone was saying was true, she said, this method of painting was an insult to women.

Shao Liuliu disagreed: "Make no mistake. A woman ordered Qi Jun to paint like this, more likely."

Voices were raised in argument, and Qi Jun held up his hands in defense. "All right. I admit, it was painted by the body of a dancer. But I wasn't there at the time. It was not done with my approval and certainly not under my direction. A woman voluntarily painted it herself, using all kinds of movements and postures. I didn't use her as a tool; in fact, you could say this is not my work. This is . . ."

Most of them didn't believe him. They thought the composition couldn't possibly be the result of fortuitous daubs and smears. People pressed him to say who it was, using what kind of "voluntary methods"? "All right, all right!" Qi Jun exclaimed. Looks like you're not going to let me off with turning over the last card in the deck." He looked at Lin Ying, as if asking for her approval.

Lin Ying was immersed in thoughts about the painting: it could be the dripping blood of a painful struggle or simply the physical record of exhibitionist, carnal dissipation. To her it represented a sudden reflexive awareness—of the final death of body and soul.

Nothing shameful here. She had no doubts. She nodded her head. She herself was no more than the artistic process. Art had transcended the observer and the tools as well and had come back to being her own.

"Please allow me to introduce the artist," Qi Jun announced momentously.

7

Qi Jun took her hand and led her in front of the painting. They made way for her to pass. He had her stand facing the painting, allowing everyone to compare her back, her buttocks, to the shapes in the painting. Then he raised both her arms in the air and slowly turned her around.

As she turned, everything in the studio whirled before her eyes, people stopped drinking and talking, all eyes were fixed on her body. The looks passed through her clothes, finding secrets that could not be displayed in front of a crowd. Why should I hide? Why be secret? After the fall of the city, with everything lost, the only thing that I have, that belongs to me, is myself. I hold just this one little bit of freedom in my hands, this pitifully small part of the right to be human. Why, on my own initiative, should I cast it off? My body and my spirit are mutually dependent means of expression— why should I fear or try to control one side of the equation?

Qi Jun put his arm around Lin Ying and said softly in her ear, "You've got to disrobe. That's the only way to show your artistry."

Eyes half closed, she did not see Qi Jun's flushed, excited face. But the idea had already been superseded by her own fierce desire. She could almost see Qi Jun's father, the owner of the apartment, frothing at the mouth. With a proud smile she signaled her agreement. Qi Jun's hand moved down her back and the zipper slid open. The dress slipped off her shoulders and down around her hips.

A pull and a stretch, and it had fallen to her feet. As usual, she was not wearing a bra. Her back was to her friends, the ridge of her spine as straight as a brush stroke. In one motion her two hands skinnied down to her waist and her bikini underpants were pushed over the curve of her buttocks. She lifted a leg, and as they fell to her feet she kicked sandals and clothes off to one side—all of this in the space of a moment.

Qi Jun steadied her, holding her arm. They were helping each other with what seemed like practiced understanding, two familiar dance partners. The young people watching were hardly breathing, as though they were watching a trapeze artist. Except for the thin white silk ribbon around her neck, Lin Ying was now totally naked.

Qi Jun dimmed the overhead lights, leaving only the wall spots shining brightly on the painting. It was as though Lin Ying had walked onto a stage. She couldn't see the faces of the audience. She had come into this world in the same attire twenty-seven years before. It had been a misty and famished, dark time, though it had been summer, like now, and should have been a dazzling golden day.

Yan Heituo pressed a button on the CD player and out of the speakers flowed a chanteuse's husky velvet voice. Lin Ying began to move, keeping time to the trumpet and the violins. Her lips were slightly open. Everything was in a haze; the light in her eyes was scorching yet indistinct, and her body felt as though it were flying.

"Let's go! Let's get out of here!" Su Jie's voice came from the doorway, furious.

She must have been trying to pull Wu Wei along with her. Muttering unintelligibly, he was helpless to resist. Hearing her, Lin Ying turned around abruptly and faced the people. Like a laser beam, their eyes fell on her breasts, then slipped down to her belly button, her private parts, taking in her whole body. The smooth rounds of her breasts were taut with fine goose bumps, making the nipples proudly erect. Her pubic hair followed the curve of her thigh, converging in the recesses underneath her smooth stomach like the veins in a leaf coming together at the stem.

Accompanied by the plaintive sound of a saxophone, the chanteuse sang with abandon, "On a summer lane, my lover was once so beautiful." The simple lyrics seemed to express the poignancy of all human life. Lin Ying stretched upward, as though she were a branch swaying slowly in the evening breeze. Her legs apart, she swayed from left to right, then back again. She felt the rotation of the entire curve of her body, she leaned her head back, her eyes still half closed, and slowly she lifted her arms. She spread her fingers and raised her wrists, making the swing of her body stretch up through her arms. Her fingers moved in a circle, their tips swirling over her head. These were the postures for "evoking the spirits," as taught by the shamans of her native southwestern land, and the hand movements were those that call down the soul. They were part of her blood, and now they came easily into her dance.

She felt a streak of rippling sparks coursing through her veins. She couldn't stop and she didn't want to stop.

"I told you not to come. But you just had to come here to see this stuff!" Su Jie couldn't maintain her dignity, and for the first time she was rebuking her husband in public. "Nothing but shameless women!" The door slammed. Instantly the room exploded with the clamor of people muttering, as if they'd woken up from a hypnotic state. Hua Hua was shouting toward the door, "What a shame. The people who should have gone are still here, and the ones who shouldn't have gone just left!" Someone else added, "The people who shouldn't have come are here, and those who should have aren't!"

Qi Jun suddenly turned off the lights entirely, leaving on only the wall spots, which he turned down to a dim glow. The room was now almost pitch-black. The signal was more than sufficient. People were busily, frantically moving about in the darkness, and they were taking off their clothes.

Shao Liuliu's tall naked body was one of the first to be seen making a leisurely circuit around the room. She stopped in front of Lin Ying, hugged her, and gave her a resounding kiss. "You're terrific. Really terrific! I hadn't imagined you'd lead the way." The music started again and Shao Liuliu gave a happy little yelp, then led Lin Ying dancing toward the middle of the room. "I've been wanting to do this for years now but never had the courage."

Lin Ying heard Li Jiangjiang in the doorway. "Friends, your little brother is in a quandary. I'm on the threshold . . . not that I'm afraid anything will happen, but . . ."

Qi Jun was trying to persuade him to stay. "We put all of this together just for you. It's to give you a send-off. Give me some face. Anyway, how can you just leave Lin Ying like this?"

"Forget it," someone else was urging Qi Jun. "Really, forget it. Don't make it hard for him." There were suggestions that Li Jiangjiang could go right to the airport and wait there, get the first ticket and just go. The night might be long, the dreams too many. "Those who can get out should tail it, fast as they can."

Lin Ying looked toward the lighted corridor. She

saw Li Jiangjiang stride out the door of the studio without so much as looking around to say good-bye to her. They heard the front door close behind him. Some people blamed Qi Jun for not knowing how to handle things. "The more you mention Lin Ying, the more he wants to go . . ."

Moving in time to the music, she went to the opposite side of the room, her back to the door. Today and from now on, I don't belong to Li Jiangjiang or to any other man. Our parting this way was unexpected but nothing to be sorry about. This way was all right. Perhaps we won't see each other after this. Go, then, go far away for as long as possible. Only then will it be truly like the reality of time—for when has time ever returned?

She remembered how she had been when she was eighteen—docile, meek, nothing but goodness in her heart. Back then she had felt the loss of something precious, but in the end it hadn't been completely without benefit. She raised her arms again, fingers pointing over her head, and her heels lifted off the ground. She felt her breasts lift up with her arms. As the beat of the music became stronger she began to dance. Her hips moved more vigorously, the thin ribbon at her neck flashed, her teeth showed—and, for the first time that night, she smiled.

8

Lin Ying relaxed against a chair by the wall, enjoying the sight of several naked couples dancing to the throbbing music. She had imagined such a scene many times in the past. Now she was seeing it with her own eyes, and it felt as though she were in a dream.

In the dimness she could just make out dark contrasting patches of pubic hair against the pale, gyrating bodies. Some of the men and women had kept their clothes on or had taken off everything but their underwear and were glued self-consciously to the wall, watching the others.

Lin Ying could see better now: Hua Hua looked rather funny, waving her arms in front of her chest, her body arched slightly backward as if she were fighting with someone; Nan An's elbows were vigorously raking back and forth at waist height, a leg thrust forward as though about to extend between Hua Hua's legs. The two of them seemed to be talking as they moved back and forth, coming teasingly closer, then moving apart again.

Near them was Shao Liuliu, her body even more beautiful than it was in clothes, with its tiny waist, broad shoulders, and full breasts. A man behind her followed her every twist and turn. From his long hair, Lin Ying knew without seeing his face that it was Qi Jun. He looked less thin than when he was fully dressed. Shao Liuliu pushed Qi Jun away from time to time, then pulled him to her, letting him accompany her in this or that movement. He stomped and he flung his hair, closely following Shao Liuliu, but in syncopation. Her exaggerated motions emphasized her astounding rear end: she was like a bounding panther, strong and sinuous. She danced easily, without inhibition, her black hair swinging around her. From time to time she let out a cry.

Lin Ying sat down, one arm resting on the chair and the other on her knee. Hua Hua passed by, sweat sparkling on her chest. She blew a kiss at Lin Ying but did not stop for a response before pirouetting and pulling another woman across the smooth floor.

A calm well-being and happiness settled on Lin Ying. She had never seen her women friends so radiant, so open, so self-confident. It was said women were born to be jealous—but not a shred of that now. Shao Liu-liu and Hua Hua, undressed, were simply far better-looking than she was: she was a southerner, with too slender and delicate a body to be fully exposed.

The long window was half open and a distant light illuminated the balcony, turning the glass of the doors into two mirrors—trees outside, an orange street lamp, pale wall lamps in the room, and dancing figures were layered on them in a montage. The off-white curtains billowed gently in the evening breeze. Lin Ying looked back and sought out the figures of the dancing women. She wondered why she had so little interest in the nakedness of the men—perhaps because they seemed so clumsy and constrained, not as natural as the women. Perhaps it was also because their nervousness made their pitiful organs dangle listlessly between their legs. Men seemed more separated from their natural state, seemed to need clothes to give themselves a front. They also seemed to fear women in this elemental condition, women who had become owners and masters of their own bodies.

She sensed a man coming in her direction. As she turned to see who it was, she was willing to hope that this man would be an exception.

9

Yan Heituo's beard was not in harmony with his naked, supple body—it was as though fake hair had been stuck on his face. His leg muscles were trembling slightly. He stood before Lin Ying's chair, looked down at her, and said, "Tired?"

"No," she said, "I'm watching. Easier to see from here."

"Tonight has opened my eyes. I've seen the unadorned image of beauty." Yan Heituo knelt on one knee to talk to her more easily. "Do you know, there's one woman here who doesn't belong to this hypocritical old world."

"Then whom does she belong to? To you?" Lin Ying asked provocatively.

"Naturally not me. She could never belong to me," he said candidly.

No suitor had ever been so frank and truthful. Lin Ying was moved. She smiled as she reached out to put her hand on his shoulder.

He grabbed hold of it. "Shall we dance?"

This attractive, talented musician had always been considerate to her, and she knew she did not really dislike him. Why then, for no apparent reason, had she never been close to him?

"With you all dressed up like that, you think we'll make a couple?" She pointed to his blue underwear.

"I just put it on. Afraid I'd make a fool of myself." Only then did she notice why he had knelt—the pants were so tight that his organ was making a ridge up the front of the fabric and, indeed, showing over the top.

"What's foolish about reproductive organs?" she said.

"Oh, well then." He stood up and stripped off his shorts. His penis immediately sprang out.

Lin Ying put her arm around his waist and they entered the dancing crowd. They were the only couple dancing together and holding on to each other. She hooked her hands behind Yan Heituo's neck and felt his skin against her breasts. Their breathing and their heartbeats responded to the sensation, and soon her breasts were pressed hard against his chest. Their thighs rubbed against each other's as his broad hand slid down the middle of her back toward her buttocks. She shut her eyes and felt a thrill of pleasure. All the muscles in her body seemed to tighten. Yan Heituo began gently to kiss her face and hair.

Do I love him? she asked herself involuntarily.

She opened her eyes and looked at him. This attractive, talented musician had always hinted that he cared about her, and she found that she did not dislike him. But for no apparent reason, she had refused to become friendly. What was happening between them now had nothing to do with conventional love, surely. Love could not be explained by reason. Whereas matters as they stood right now could be explained quite easily, could be arranged, could be induced. They were rationally related to lust, a fundamental component of human nature.

Human nature. Pure and unadulterated. Nature in its purity.

In this era of inhuman behavior, I will follow the dictates of nature's desire.

Her hair had long since fallen loose around her face.

Tossing it back, she noticed that the nude dancers all around were watching the two of them. Was she again leading the way? Yan Heituo's heart was pounding madly against her chest. She slowly pulled the white ribbon from around her neck and allowed it to flutter to the ground. Her arm went around his waist and she smoothly leaned back until her body was curved in the line of an arc. Her nipples, looking as though gilded with ochre, were so full they felt as if they would split.

Yan Heituo bent over her and pressed his face against her breast, then lightly bit the concentration of redness in the middle. Her heart flew upward even as her body moved, irresistibly, to the floor. The muscles in her pelvis were throbbing fiercely. Surging desire made her body feel empty. She had never before so ached for union with another body.

Do it right here, under everyone's staring eyes? Perhaps her desire was so intense precisely because everyone was staring. There was no need for her to be first, but she rejoiced for her own sake that she could enter this realm at all. The lips of her vulva gently kissed his penis as though a key were easily turning in a door and behind that door all the tense taboos were springing out and away. Her tongue was burning fiercely, her throat was dry. She opened her mouth and began to pant.

"Look what it's come to! If they were all like you, you ne'er-do-well, this country would be impossible to keep under control. If you don't bring credit to my name, take over properly—those decadent counter-revolutionaries will overturn heaven itself."

She could hold back no longer. Vehemently she

raised her left leg and clamped it over Yan Heituo's body. In that instant, her warm, moist lips were filled, blocked. She flowed with strangely hot juices as a long, hard thing was pulled into her body. She cried out sharply as the two of them came together. Stars rose like fireworks before her eyes, exploding in the air, turning into golden rain, falling throughout the sky.

10

Lin Ying heard the music change.

She suddenly became aware that the person holding her now, caressing her most sensitive parts, was another man, one who had not declared himself to her, who had not even come after her or pursued her. After she and Yan Heituo had fallen to the ground and felt their senses explode within her, she had rolled out of his embrace. When had this other one came over to her?

All the lights were now out. The sky had turned indigo. The lights of another building, street lamps, and the occasional car brought an intermittent gleam into the dark apartment. A bluish glow spilled out over the naked bodies lying on its floor.

Who are you?

She wanted to ask but didn't. What should I do, she wondered, yell or resist? A man should at least ask if he intends to be intimate with a woman.

She rolled over on top of this man and straightened up to look around. By the window light she could see quite a few embracing men and women, some on the sofa, some leaning against the walls, more on the terrazzo floor, connected to each other in every conceivable posture. A sustained sound of heavy breathing filled the air, punctuated from time to time by a cry of pleasure or pain. From the sounds, she could tell that the intertwined legs right next to her were those of Hua Hua. She reached across to caress her, and Hua Hua cried in excitement, her body moving ever more violently. She seemed happy that Lin Ying was watching her make love like this, right in front of her, and perhaps she had put herself here intentionally, so Lin could watch.

Why is it that women are the ones who give permission? And why do they think it is they who will lose something? Men are the ones who really lose out, Lin Ying thought. Do I really need to know the man I make love to? Fact is, there's no need for me to know anything about him.

Sex should not concern itself with anything but sex. Like now: whether she knew this man under her or not, she was equally glad to regard him as a stranger. At this moment, she wanted the feeling of strangeness, a brand-new feeling. She grabbed his hair, bent over, and slowly pressed her body to his—not to please him but to satisfy herself.

Physical pleasure between a man and a woman can reach a kind of ultimate happiness if it is unsullied by the conditions of civilized man. Sex can bring the great relief of going past the messy bonds and boundaries of social relationships. Those who don't dare to put their feet in this river lose something fundamental. Their associations become merely for-profit transactions, carefully considered speculative investments in this or that kind of business; no wonder their relationships founder in the muck of jealousy. The moment sex is a bargaining chip, it becomes a tool of repression and control. Promises of love, fidelity, and sacrifice that sound sacred in the making are actually selfish displays of raw possession—fraudulent, outside the purity of sex, deceiving of oneself and others. The evidence is apparent all over: every couple, however happy to start with, sooner or later find themselves loathing these things and tormenting or betraying each other in revenge.

You're lucky, she said to herself. Tonight you have cast it all off. At least you can say proudly, I am freer than ever before. No longer the slave of my own body.

Excited again by these thoughts, she parted her legs. Something hot pressed against her labia, lingered there a moment, then slipped in like a tongue of flame licking into her body. This was all so familiar that she called out with surprised pleasure. The bottom part of her body was burning, swelling. She moaned, and gradually the pain turned into long-awaited abandon. Tears coursed down her face as the two of them rolled over, and the boundless universe spun on its axis in the wetness of their bodies and faces.

She gripped his head, unwilling to open her eyes to make any kind of affirmation or denial. Her vibrating body was dotted with sky-blue marks, shiny with a hard, transparent luster. Beads of sweat rolled sideways down her thighs, tender delicate glints coursing across her skin.

Her fingers gripped his buttocks as their tongues wound around each other, like the lips of her vagina tightly sucking at his penis. She brought one leg down from over his hips and inserted it between his two legs, so that his penis could be more deeply planted in her. She wanted to swallow up his entire sex, take the feeling of fulfillment forever into her body. A man, a woman, no name, no person.

She felt her vagina contracting, coming in spasms, violently shaking her entire body with intoxicating pain. When she could bear it no longer she rolled to stretch out on top of him, her mouth sealing his to hold back his howl. From the root of her groin came pounding waves of pleasure, violently throwing them both into the depths. Her body now became supremely light and tensile, as though she were walking on the avenue, where the sun had brought the flowers into full bloom, as though she were walking in a profusion of joy.

Each position they used was a kind of prayer. She had become art, the art of sex, its lyrics. Her body, fully revealed, was as pure and unblemished from top to bottom as her eyes. In rhythm with the other now, her body was shaking. A high-pitched shout was searching for her response. In the moment that her breathing almost stopped, the two of them spurted into a liquid state, melting together to become one.

11

The sharp crack of a knock came from the door. Loud and urgent.

Stunned silence. Nobody knew what to do.

Qi Jun quickly pulled on his trousers and strode across the hallway. "Who is it?" he asked through the door. An answer came from the other side. He spun around to face the black recesses of the painting studio and barked in a low voice: "Police!"

He flicked on a light. After a second of paralysis, people leapt up, scrambling to find their clothes. Someone started straightening the chairs.

The knocking grew louder, and shouts came that the door was going to be smashed in. Qi Jun made a quieting motion with his hands. Then he calmly and leisurely opened the door, welcoming the visitors in a normal tone of voice.

Four or five policemen stalked in. They stood for a moment in the hallway. You could tell at a glance that the younger-looking one was the leader. He led the others in, across the hall, then from room to room. There were empty beer bottles on the floor by the walls, some half empty. "What's going on here?" he snapped, his voice savage, as if he were interrogating a criminal. "So many people!"

"Party. Sending off a friend." Qi Jun gave a little laugh as he said it.

"We were alerted by a phone call. What you have here is an assembly that contravenes the Martial Law Edict. We're in a Special Martial Law Period after the Riot. Don't you know that? More than three people get together and you need permission from the local police station!" They had entered the studio. The people inside had already put on their clothes, and some of the women, standing behind the men, were smoothing their hair.

Qi Jun looked around quickly. Nothing suspicious —everything looked passably covered up. The music was still on. He resumed the haughty demeanor of the son of a high-ranking general. "Weather's hot, a few friends got together to drink some beer. We told the police station beforehand. Very sorry to have caused you so much trouble." Then he stopped. His jaw dropped as he looked across the room, speechless. The officer and two policemen were as stunned as he.

Lin Ying stood at the far end of the room, as naked as she had been before. Each person had been busy worrying about himself, not noticing that, off in a corner she refused to get dressed.

She stood absolutely erect, her hair hanging to her shoulders. One leg was slightly forward, her heel raised slightly off the ground, her two hands resting in a natural pose on her thigh, right hand lightly touching the left wrist. Under the unaccustomed bright light, she faced everyone straight on, including the immaculately attired policemen. Her nipples and pubic hair were exposed, without the slightest attempt at concealment. Her face wore a serene smile, exactly as it had when everything began earlier in the evening.

"Oh, my heavens, she's gone crazy!" Hua Hua and Shao Liuliu cried out together. Yan Heituo grabbed some clothes and charged over to her.

Without changing expression, she brushed them aside. Just at that moment the music changed to a percussive rhythmic beat. She began to sway in time to it, slowly, lithely, taking two beats to one. Her hands now crossed over each other as she raised her arms, fingers gently undulating overhead.

"What kind of party is this?" The officer whipped around to Qi Jun.

Qi Jun hastily explained that the woman had mental problems, was prone to epileptic fits in which she would suddenly peel off her clothes. Best thing would be to let a couple of her lady friends take her off to another room to rest. Qi Jun walked over to stand in front of her, so that she was cut her off from the policemen's line of vision. Somebody turned the music off.

Lin Ying stepped around him, and went on dancing, humming to herself now as she slowly moved forward. As she danced, she said inside, *I will not change. There is no power on earth that can make me change.*

The policemen started pushing people to one side of the room. "Against the wall! Stand up against the wall!" The huge painting on the wall had fallen and was being trampled under the policemen's feet. Perhaps they didn't even realize it was a painting. Lin Ying was now standing by herself in the center of the room. She lowered her head to look down at the painting, and when she looked up again her eyes clashed with those of a young policeman.

A uniformed man pushed a few people rudely aside, leaned down, and gathered up an armful of clothes from a chair, women's and men's all mixed together. He carried them over to the officer, who wrinkled his nose in disgust.

"All right, just exactly what is going on here?" came the command.

Qi Jun talked fast as he led the officer into the adjoining room. They seemed to be making a telephone call. Qi Jun and the officer took turns explaining. Some people wanted to leave but were blocked by policemen at the door. One officer undid the electric cudgel at his waist and played with it in his hands. People looked at one another, shocked, too scared to speak, the faces of some white with terror. Everyone tried hard not to watch Lin Ying, still naked and dancing by herself. The young policeman had delicate features, but his eyes were cold and his face was absolutely impassive.

Qi Jun's voice rose, then dropped again. After a moment, he said, "All right. Fine."

Lin Ying thought she had never been happier than at this moment, facing the policeman with his loaded gun. She knew that her nudity no longer meant sex to anyone, that her flesh and her licentious dance were only making people uncomfortable. Most of them were probably upset, blaming her for bringing trouble on everyone. Or perhaps they really thought she had gone crazy. She didn't need to explain anything to anyone: whether they understood or not had nothing to do with her.

When the word *Police* had hissed through the room and people had plunged for their clothes, trying to cover themselves, she had known theirs was a natural, spontaneous reaction, something she would have done herself before. But in that instant she made a decision: I will never again hide in the face of violence. From this moment on, my running is over.

From the next room came the sound of the receiver being put down. Shortly after, the telephone rang and Qi Jun answered. He said a few words and then passed the phone to the officer. "They want to talk to you."

The officer, supremely unhappy, was saying, "Yes, all right. Well then, that's what we'll do." He put down the phone and stormed into the studio. He went straight to Lin Ying, opened his mouth, and yelled at her, "Put on your clothes!"

Qi Jun was holding a nightgown. He walked around

the officer and put it over her shoulders, not daring to look Lin Ying in the face. In that second she understood: with the intervention of Qi Jun's father, her friends had once again slipped by. For the time being, at least, they would be free to go, but she would be receiving different treatment. With a flick of her shoulder she let the nightgown fall to the floor.

"Put on your clothes, you shameless whore!"

Her face was as serene as before but no longer smiling. The officer undid the handcuffs fastened at his waist and announced to her in a loud, ceremonious voice, "You have committed the crime of indecent behavior. By Article 169 of the criminal code of the People's Republic of China and by the edict on martial law promulgated by the municipality of Beijing, I, representing the Public Security Bureau of the western district of Beijing City, hereby take you under arrest."

Lin Ying put her hands straight out in front of her for him to handcuff. The officer motioned to another policeman to dress her, but her hands stayed rigidly stretched before him; she was refusing to let them put on the clothes.

"Get dressed!" The officer's voice almost broke in his hysteria. This woman was intending to challenge his authority! He raised his fist at her and was about to hit her when he caught himself and instead, with practiced, sure movements, clapped the handcuffs on her wrists.

"Let's go," she said quietly. This was the first time she had spoken. She turned to the others. Their faces, at the other end of the room, showed shock, horror, sorrow, sympathy. Some of her friends had tears in their eyes. The wailing of police sirens in the street now penetrated the room. Lin Ying turned back to the front door without nodding in farewell. She had already entered a new realm where none of them was willing to follow.

The policeman draped the nightgown over her back. Barefoot, she walked through the door.

1 2

The nightmares will soon be over, she thought.

She raised her head. The summer night's sky was already showing a faint glimmer of dawn. A paddy wagon was parked on the empty street. Nobody was around to watch, although people woken by the sirens may have been looking out from behind curtained windows. On the walls were the ineradicable traces of slogans from the long history of one political storm after another. She stepped into the wagon and sat down on the seat. The skin on the back of her legs flinched from the cold metal where it wasn't protected by the nightgown. As she sat, she placed her handcuffed hands gently on her knees.

She heard strains of music as the vehicle started up, heard the unrestrained power of a beat pounding at her from the distance, carrying in its teeth the lines of a poem. It was like the dawn, settling down over this city, arrogant, calm, assured.

Have you thought about the terrifying word *life*?
In the chilled flames,

It's better to let a *tan*-flower* bear the burden of responsibility for you.

She felt sort of hungry.

August–December 1991

<hr />

* *Tan*-flower, Chinese for the night-blooming cereus, Sanskrit *udumbara*, a
flower that blooms only once for a few hours on a summer night. According
to the Buddhist Scripture *Saddharmapundarikasutra*, the flower blooms only
when the Sacred King Cakravartirajan comes again to the human world.